Clutch Hitter!

It was the bottom of the eighth, the Elmira Sox down 3–0 to the St. Catherines Blue Jays. With two outs and the bases loaded, the Sox dugout was alive, screaming for a rally.

"Now batting for the Sox . . . David Green!" the P.A. announced.

David dug in at the plate and waited. The pitcher went into his stretch and fired low and away.

Ball one.

The next pitch was wildly high, forcing the catcher to reach over his head to grab it.

Ball two.

"They're gonna walk him with the bases loaded and give us a token run," gasped the Elmira coach, "rather than risk a grand slam!"

David saw the next pitch coming, a waist-high fastball almost a foot off the outside corner of the plate. For anyone else it would be another ball. But it looked good enough to David.

He went into his power swing and connected with a solid crack!

Other books in the ROOKIES series:

Rookies
SQUEEZE PLAY

Mark Freeman

BALLANTINE BOOKS ● NEW YORK

Special thanks to Mark L. Crose

RLI: VL: 6 & up
      IL: 6 & up

Library of Congress Catalog Card Number: 88-92817

ISBN 0-345-35903-8

Manufactured in the United States of America

First Edition: June 1989
Third Printing: April 1990

For my best friend, Susan

ROOKIES
Squeeze Play

ONE

David Green stood with one foot in and one foot out of the batter's box. He lifted the navy blue cap, with its scarlet-and-white B, and wiped the nervous perspiration from his forehead. Looking down the third-base line, he got his sign from the Red Sox' coach and stepped back to the plate.

"C'mon, Green," he told himself as he glared out at the mound. "Just hang in there. . . . You can do it. . . . You've got to do it!"

The Detroit Tigers' ace pitcher, Jack Morris, stared down at him from the mound. Brushing his long moustache with his fingers, Morris took his grip on the baseball and seemed to laugh at his young opponent. The crowd's roar increased to deafening levels as he went into his stretch.

David caught the scoreboard out of the corner of his eye. He didn't need the reminder that Boston was behind 6–3. He knew this was it . . . the bottom of the ninth . . . two outs . . . a three-ball-and-two-strike count.

Morris checked the runners, one at each base, and then focused on his catcher's target. Winding up, his arm whipped forward, unleashing the vicious fastball for the inside corner of the plate.

David's eyes watched each rotation of the ball as it spun toward him. It seemed as if everything was moving in slow motion. Even before he started his swing, he thought, *This can't be happening . . . Jack Morris doesn't screw up!*

The pitch was right in David's power alley. His body coiled tightly and released in perfect rhythm. The bat flashed around, crossed the plate, and caught the ball right at the full release of his strength.

Morris spun around and stared as the ball rocketed off David's bat. The infield turned, but too late to pick up the trajectory of the shot. The Tiger outfielders didn't even move.

David dropped his bat at the plate and stood in the batter's box watching. He gazed as the ball rose up over the light poles in straightaway center field and then disappeared into the chilly Boston night.

The crowd erupted in a frenzied cheer. The public-address announcer shouted, "Boston wins . . . seven to six . . . Unbelievable . . . Boston wins!"

The chant went up in the stands, "DT! DT! DT! DT!"

As he circled the bases in his very best home-run trot, David faintly heard a voice rise up above the crowd's explosive screams.

"David?" the plaintive voice cried out.

David searched the stands, trying to pinpoint the voice.

"David? . . ." the voice seemed louder. "David . . . are you up yet?"

Shaking the cobwebs from his mind, David made the last cruel step back into consciousness. He opened his eyes and strained to look around his room. Blinking back reality, he slowly sat up in his bed.

"You'd better get a move on, David," his mother said as she poked her head around his bedroom door. "You don't want to miss the plane, do you?"

"Is it that late?" he yelled as he leaped out of his bed and hit the floor. "I can't believe I slept that long."

The pulsating hot water from the shower completed the job of waking David up physically. But his mind continued to drift. He wasn't aware of washing his hair as his thoughts centered on the past.

It's hard to believe four years have gone by, he reflected to himself. *It's gonna be hard to*

*beat the time I've had at good ol' Rosemont
High. I hope I'm doing the right thing.*

Today, he was heading off to a new life. A life
he had only dreamed about before. Having just
signed a contract with the Boston Red Sox to
play professional baseball, David was starting
to feel insecure about his decision. And one of
the hardest things he faced was saying good-bye
to his friends.

Slapping the faucet handle shut, David
grabbed a towel and dried himself off. He wiped
the mirror clear and strained to see his reflec-
tion through the thick water vapor. "At least
we're all taking off together," he consoled himself.

The Los Angeles Dodgers had drafted his
fireballing friend, Roberto Ramirez. Glen Mitchell, his other best friend, had been taken by the
Chicago White Sox. The whole town of Rosemont, as well as the rest of the nation, had been
shocked when three players off the same high
school team were drafted to play professional
baseball at the same time.

As he went into his bedroom to finish packing, David was suddenly hit with the awesome
reality of the situation. Throwing some more
shirts into his suitcase, he looked around his
room and sighed. "Well, it won't be long
now. . . . I'm gonna be completely on my
own!"

He shook his head as he left his bedroom and
wondered when he'd be back.

* * *

Chicago's O'Hare Airport was a confusing tangle of terminals and corridors. Rosa and Carlos Ramirez wandered down the long walkways, searching for gate 72. Roberto had his nose buried in a map as he walked. He still wasn't sure exactly where Salem, Oregon was located.

Roberto's life had been a whirlwind since being drafted by the Los Angeles Dodgers. Friends, relatives, newspapermen, and television people had kept him constantly on the centerstage. He was almost looking forward to the time alone he would have on the plane.

At least I'll have a chance to find out what's close to Salem, he thought to himself as he thumbed through his travel atlas and picked his way through the crowd.

"Robbie, are you sure it was gate seventy-two we were supposed to meet them at?" a harassed Rosa Ramirez asked her son.

"Yeah, Mom. I'm sure. I'm positive, Glen wouldn't screw that up."

All three of Rosemont's new celebrities were leaving on the same day for their new careers in baseball. Glen was headed for Utica, New York; David was on his way to Elmira, New York; and Roberto was going to the other side of the country: Salem, Oregon.

They had agreed to meet at the airport for one final farewell. The boys had put off talking about their separation, always feeling in the back of their mind that it wasn't really happening. As Roberto heard the roar of the jet engines on the sleek white airplanes, he knew that the time was near.

The Ramirez family was startled when they heard a yell down the aisle. "Magic . . . down here!"

An excited Glen was thrilled to see his teammate and buddy. Slapping him on the back, he said, "I was starting to think you weren't gonna make it. What took you so long?"

Roberto folded up his maps and stuffed them in his carry bag. "I had a heckuva time figuring out everything I needed to take. Then I had to put back half the stuff I wanted. I can't believe how little room I have for everything."

Glen nodded. "I know what ya mean." Shaking his head and whispering, he continued, "This is really weird, isn't it? I mean, I can't believe we're actually going."

Catching his family out of the corner of his eye, Roberto silently nodded.

The two boys stood for a moment, lost for words, wondering what to do or say. A hard slap on their shoulders shocked them both silly.

"Geez, Green," Glen said, smiling, "Give us a warning next time, will ya?"

David had spotted his two friends talking and decided to sneak up from behind and surprise them. "Sorry, guys. I didn't know you were so uptight, Scraps." David looked into their eyes, then lowered his own voice. "I thought I was gonna be the only one who might be upset by all of this."

Roberto smashed forearms with David in their time-honored Rosemont tradition. "Hey, pal. This is a big deal. I'm not afraid to admit I'm a little scared."

"Yeah. Me, too," Glen said.

David saw all the parents gather together in the waiting area to talk. He pulled his friends off down the concourse. "C'mon, you guys. Let's go get something to drink. I'm dying."

"Great. I could use a shot of something myself," said Glen.

The boys walked silently down the crowded corridor. Roberto watched as the people around him trudged off, head down, making their way to a thousand different destinations. He noticed that people coming off arriving flights seemed happier than those headed for departing flights. He decided that it was probably in his own head.

Uncomfortable from the long silence between them, Roberto poked his friends and said, "Hey, isn't anybody gonna say anything? I mean, I don't know what to do. . . . I feel real strange. . . . Don't you guys?"

"Yeah. *Real* strange!" Glen said. "This isn't like I thought it was gonna be."

The three boys got in line at the snack bar.

"I thought I'd be okay about it, and in a way I am . . ." Glen continued, grabbing a soda from the rack. "But I'm gonna miss you guys, and I guess I don't know what else to say."

David wadded up the paper from his straw and loaded it into firing position. When he heard Glen's words, he dropped the straw and took a sip of his cola. "Yeah. Maybe this is what growing up's all about."

"I wish you guys weren't headed way out there in New York," Roberto sighed as he took a long swallow of his Seven-Up. "I'm the one who's gonna be out in the Northwest League. At least you guys will get to see each other once in a while."

David looked at Glen. "I wonder if we'll get to play each other? Whaddaya know about the New York–Penn League anyway?"

Glen shook his head. "Not much. All I know is Elmira and Utica are both in New York. Don't ask me where or how far apart." Glen took the last swallow of his drink and crushed the paper cup into a ball. "But I figure we must play each other maybe ten, twelve times during the season."

Without looking up from the table, David said, "Well, at least that'll be ten, twelve wins our team can expect."

Glen flung his wadded cup at his buddy. "In your dreams, Green. I'm never gonna let your pathetic team beat me at anything."

"Who's talking pathetic? You don't know anything about the Elmira Red Sox," David proudly pointed out.

"They're gonna be stuck with you, that's all I need to know." The hairs on the back of Glen's neck were starting to rise. Always competitive, he was ready to argue for his team even though he knew nothing about it.

Roberto glanced at his watch and smiled. He searched for a display terminal in the hallway next to the snack bar. Double-checking his departure time, he stood and pushed the chair away from the table.

"Well, guys. I think this is it. I've gotta get going."

The harsh reality of leaving was hitting home hard. Roberto's eyelids started to feel heavy, and he had difficulty blinking.

The brief verbal battle between his two friends reminded Roberto that the spirit of competition was burning bright. *That's one of the things I love the most about baseball,* he thought to himself. *Laying it on the line and fighting to win.*

As the three ex-teammates walked back up the concourse toward their waiting planes, they stopped and dropped their bags. Putting their hands out together, one on top of the other, David, Roberto, and Glen shared one last moment together.

"Good luck, guys," Roberto said.

"Hey, man . . . you, too." Glen couldn't think of anything else to say.

David turned from one friend to the other. He felt the tension and anxiety. Slapping them both on the arm, he laughed and said, "Hey. This is only gonna be three months. We can stay in touch by phone, and we'll all meet back here in September. No sweat, right?"

Roberto and Glen grinned and nodded.

"The important thing—play well and have fun, okay?" David said, reaching for his bag.

They all breathed a sigh of relief.

As Roberto walked toward his family and his plane to Oregon, he made one final turn and called out, "First one to the majors buys."

Glen yelled across the waiting area, "Buys what?"

Roberto waved him off. "We'll figure that out later," he said as he disappeared down Gate 72's ramp.

TWO

Peering out the tiny airplane window next to him, Dave Green searched for a familiar landmark below. The clear skies provided him with a fantastic view. He wished he had studied geography a little harder now that he had the chance to appreciate it.

That's gotta be Lake Erie, he said to himself, his excitement building as the waters beneath him stretched as far as he could see. He fumbled through the pouch in front of him, looking for a flight map to see how close he was to Buffalo now.

The Boston Red Sox scout, Walt Charles, had given David detailed instructions for his trip. It was his job to make sure that David arrived safely in Elmira. After that, the club would take care of everything.

After he landed at Buffalo, New York, David took a cab to the downtown bus station and boarded a Greyhound headed to Elmira through the western part of the state. Covering the 150-mile trip in a little over three hours, David arrived in Elmira in the late afternoon, tired and hungry.

As he wandered around the tiny bus depot, David started to feel lonely. He tried to focus on his goal: to play major-league baseball.

"What a dump!" David muttered under his breath as he stood in the only waiting area the station had. Someone was supposed to meet him there, and was late. He decided that he'd give the guy ten more minutes, then he'd go off to discover exciting Elmira on his own. He plopped down in one of the old, rickety wood seats and picked up a local newspaper left on the chair beside him. He searched for the sports section but couldn't find it. "Probably not much goin' on, anyway," he grumbled as he flipped the paper away from him.

Just as he was about to stand and leave, he heard a voice from behind call out, "Dave Green?"

"Yo!" David responded, jumping to attention and spinning around to find who was speaking.

A tall, dark-haired man, approximately twenty-five to thirty years old, stood in the center of the station. His warm smile and con-

fident gray eyes made David feel at ease. He
walked toward David and extended his hand.

"Hi, I'm Jeff Fox. I'm here on behalf of the ball
club to pick you up and help get you situated."

The two shook hands, the strength of their
grip increasing in a brief test. "I'm real glad to
see you. I wasn't sure where to go from here."

Jeff laughed. "Well, that's my job. As director
of player personnel, assistant equipment manager, tour guide, chauffeur, part-time general
manager, scoreboard operator, senior vice-
president, and . . . occasional chief executive
officer, I'm supposed to take care of you and get
you settled properly here in Elmira."

"Geez, it sounds like you've got a lot of jobs
on the team."

"Actually, what I really am is the owner's son.
And in the minor leagues the owner is respon-
sible for everything I mentioned, so . . . here I
am."

"Great!" David blurted out.

"Let me help you with your bags," Jeff said as
he reached for David's suitcase. "As you've
probably already figured out by the salary
you're gonna be paid, there isn't much money to
be had in the New York–Penn League. So we all
work everywhere we can to cut corners and
make ends meet."

As they walked out of the old train station,
David squinted into the early-evening sun. Red
brick buildings rose up all around him. There
was a surprising number of maple and oak trees

scattered throughout the area, giving the city a comfortable, homey atmosphere.

"Looks like a nice, quiet town."

"Yeah, I guess you're right. Too quiet here during the winter."

David was amazed at how few people he saw on the streets. "Seems like a weird place for a baseball franchise. How many fans do you get anyway?"

"The crowds aren't big, but they're loyal and can be pretty outspoken. A team like this, everyone feels like they can run it."

Jeff threw David's bag in the trunk of his car. "Well, anyway, let's get you a room at the Country Squire. It's close to the ball park and handy to everything you'll need. Most of the players stay there, and I think you'll like it."

David shrugged. "Whatever you say. You're the boss."

"After that, let's grab a bite to eat and then hit the ol' ball park. Game time's eight o'clock."

David stared at him for a minute in disbelief. "You mean I've got a game tonight? Already?"

"The Sox do. I don't think that Johnny would play you tonight. But you might as well get introduced and—if that's okay?" Jeff noticed the stunned look on David's face.

"Oh, no . . . that's great. I was just surprised that there'd be a game tonight. I just left Rosemont this morning and . . . well . . . I guess I wasn't thinking."

As they climbed into Jeff's perfectly preserved, cherry red '67 Mustang, the owner's son slapped David on the back. "Hey, don't sweat it. We've been going at it for three weeks already. The manager, Johnny Sullivan, will break you in slowly . . . give you time to get your feet on the ground—all of three minutes flat."

David felt embarrassed. "Hey, I'm ready. If Elmira's got a game tonight, I'll do whatever the coach wants."

Jeff nodded. "Great. But first things first. Let's get you into that hotel, and then, food."

"Sounds good to me," David said. "I'm starving."

He looked out the window of Jeff's Mustang as they drove through Elmira. He saw the mixture of old and new buildings and tried to guess what kind of city it was.

For a second he reflected back on Rosemont. The two cities were about the same population, he guessed. They seemed to him to be about the same age. He wondered how similar they were going to be.

The sun was framed just above the top of Harris Hill when Jeff Fox wheeled his Mustang into the Elmira Red Sox' baseball park. David whipped his head around in a circle, trying to take in everything he could see.

The ball field was little more than a county park with bleachers for about four thousand people. There was one building that served the multiple purpose of housing the offices, club-house, concession stands, and control tower for the lights and scoreboard. David thought back to his last game in Civic Stadium in Chicago and winced. He glanced at his watch and turned to Jeff.

"Seven-ten. Are we still okay?" he asked, getting out of the car.

"Relax. It's your first day, so no one expects you to be on a regular schedule yet. Just let me introduce you to everyone and . . ." Jeff stopped in midsentence.

"Yeah?"

Laughing, Jeff pushed him in the direction of the clubhouse. "I was gonna tell you not to let anyone bother you."

"Whaddaya mean?"

"Well, you're the new kid, don't forget. There's bound to be a certain amount of testing, resentment . . . you know."

David rolled his eyes. He thought back to the pranks Scrapper Mitchell used to pull back home on new guys. "Yeah. I guess I've got some of that coming. We used to bug the sophomores and juniors. . . ."

"Yeah, well," Fox said, smiling, "Remember this is pro ball."

"So?"

"So, you need to realize that if you come on the team, do well, and start playing all the time, you're taking someone else's *job* away from them. Sometimes, the competition can get crazy." Jeff let his words sink in. "Get the picture? You're a threat to some of these guys. Don't expect them to welcome you with open arms."

David stiffened. "You make it sound like it's gonna be a war in there."

"No, but it's tough. You come in, show 'em what you can do, earn their respect, and then gradually start hanging out with the guys who are in the same boat as you."

David rubbed his neck and shook his head. Another hard reality was hitting him between the eyes. "I never thought about that," he said. "And I could even get fired and sent packing."

Jeff swung open the door to the main building. "That's something that's always hanging over you. Don't think about it, or it'll happen. But don't forget about it, either. You've got to always remember, you're only as good as your latest stats. Nobody here cares about anything that happened before."

"Is there anything I should know about the manager? What did you say his name was . . . Johnny . . .?"

"Sullivan. Johnny Sullivan. Real straight-up guy. You won't ever have to worry about him. You'll always know exactly where you stand with him."

"That's good," David sighed as he nervously wiped his brow.

"Just give him all you've got all the time, and you've got nothing to sweat." Jeff held open the clubhouse door and pointed David in the right direction. "C'mon. Let's get you ready."

The Elmira locker room hit David with all the familiar smells and sounds that surround a baseball team. Immediately he felt more at ease.

Jeff led him over to a tall, lanky man with wavy salt-and-pepper-colored hair. He appeared to be in his late forties, early fifties to David.

"Johnny, I want to introduce you to our new recruit, Dave Green." Jeff's words made Sullivan's eyebrows rise.

"So . . . you got me some left-handed power, finally." Sullivan extended an open hand to David. "Glad you're here, Green."

David shook his hand and gulped. "Glad to meet you, Mr. Sullivan. I hope—"

"Johnny. Just call me Johnny. We don't stand on formalities around here."

David felt the eyes of all the other players on him. "Okay, Johnny. I'm happy to be here."

"C'mon. Follow me," Sullivan said as he walked toward the wall of open-stalled cubicles. "This'll be your locker." The space was right in the middle of the clubhouse. "I hope the uniform fits okay . . . it's the best we could do. I'll introduce you to everyone as soon as you suit up."

Without another word, Sullivan turned and walked back toward his office. David froze for a moment, thinking that there was something more to say or do. When he saw Jeff walking out the door, he knew he was on his own now.

Dropping his bag in front of the narrow cubicle, David lifted the gray uniform from the rack. He held it up and spun it around to check out the number on the back.

Seven! I can live with that, he thought as he slowly unbuttoned the well-worn jersey. The two-color navy-and-scarlet lettering on the front neatly spelled out Elmira in script form. His navy blue hat had a scarlet-and-white S on the front . . . for Sox.

After he pulled up his pants and adjusted his stirrup socks, he fished his cleats out of his bag and found his trusty A2000 glove. He wondered if he should go up to some of the other players and introduce himself, but he stopped himself when he realized he didn't know what to say.

When most of the other players started wandering out of the clubhouse toward the field, David fell in behind them. When he entered the passageway to the dugout and got his first glimpse at the playing field, David felt a lump form in his throat.

Already out on the field, the Oneonta Yankees, dressed in the famous navy blue pinstripes of their parent club, were warming up. The stands were almost filled and the organist was playing a medley of Broadway hits.

Peanut vendors were working the stands, and the bright lights high above the field cast a yellow glow over the park. The scoreboard out in center field, covered with local sponsors' names, proudly explained that this was the home ball park of the Elmira Red Sox.

David stood frozen in time at the foot of the dugout stairs as he slowly turned and soaked in every detail of his surroundings. In some strange way, it was everything he'd ever thought it might be.

His manager came up behind him and pushed him up the stairs toward the playing field. "You'd better get warmed up, kid, just in case."

David stumbled up the steps and spun back toward his coach. In an awkward attempt to ask where to go, he said, "Where am I?"

Sullivan stared at him and shook his head. "Hey, kid, wake up. You're in the minor league."

THREE

Glen Mitchell strolled out on the neatly mani-cured baseball field and immediately headed for second base. He checked out the ground around the bag like a doctor examining his patient. After kicking the white canvas base and watch-ing the dust fly, he announced to no one in particular, "Not bad. Not bad at all!"

Having just arrived in Utica, New York, Glen's mind was already focused on the most impor-tant thing in his life: playing pro ball. He couldn't wait to get started. He'd examined the area around his playing position even before he'd gone into the locker room to get his gear.

After his introduction in the clubhouse, Glen sat down at his locker and started pulling on his baseball gear. The player next to him started up a conversation.

"Hi, guy. Mitchell, right?"

Glen extended his hand. "Right. Glen Mitchell."

"Steve Lang. Where ya from?"

"Chicago area . . . a little suburb called Rosemont." Glen eyed his interrogator carefully. "How 'bout you?"

"Garden Grove, California. What position ya play?"

Glen sensed this was more than idle chitchat. "Second base."

Lang's raised eyebrows told Glen he didn't have to ask his position.

"You must be just outta high school then, right?" Lang asked nervously.

"Yep. How long have you been playing?"

"This is my second year."

Glen rolled his eyes. "Long time, huh?" As soon as he said it he wished he hadn't.

Lang's back straightened and his voice lowered to a growl. "Hey, kid. Don't think you can come flying through here on a first-class ticket. I had to wait my turn, and so will you. You're gonna be playing behind me. I'm at second base."

"Hey, okay. I know." Glen finished buttoning his navy blue jersey and reached up for his hat. "C'mon. You can do me a big favor and show me the ropes around here. I'm just trying to learn what the heck I'm supposed to do. Whaddaya say?"

Lang stood up and punched Glen in the arm a little harder than he needed to, but Glen didn't say anything. "Okay, kid. Let's go," he said, and walked toward the door.

The Utica White Sox had already been playing for a month. When Glen joined the other players out in the field for pregame warm-ups, it was obvious that things had not been going well. Their manager, Ted Holmes, was barking instructions, and tension showed on all the players' faces.

Glen stood next to Lang beside the batting cage as they waited their turn for hitting practice. Glen said, "What's the team's record so far this season?"

Lang leaned forward and half whispered, "Five and seventeen."

Glen whistled and shook his head. "I guess that's why the coach seems pretty uptight."

"Yeah. And it's been getting worse every game. Last season here wasn't any great shakes. I was hoping to get a fast start this year and maybe get moved up to double A."

Glen cocked his head toward Lang. "And? How's it going?"

Utica's starting second baseman just shook his head.

Glen swung his weighted bat around and over his head and then tossed it to the ground. He grabbed his regular-size bat and stepped into the cage. He yelled back to Lang, "If we get a couple of wins in a row, everything will change."

"Stop flapping your lips and get in there," the Utica manager yelled from out on the mound. He was standing behind a screen setup for the batting-practice pitcher and had been watching his hitters carefully.

Holmes turned to his pitcher and said, "Let's see what the new kid's got. Bear down a little on him."

Glen scraped a foothold with his cleats and slapped his batting helmet down on his head. He watched the pitcher's delivery and then cracked a line drive into left field on the first pitch.

Two more pitches and two more solid hits caught the attention of everyone on the field. Holmes growled at his pitcher, "Throw him some curves and screwballs. Anyone can hit a fastball."

Glen rapped the next two pitches sharply into center field, the second hit whizzing right over the manager's head.

"Not bad. Next!" Holmes shouted.

Steve Lang watched the action closely and grudgingly complimented Glen as he walked by. "Good job, Mitchell."

"Thanks."

"Game pitching won't be that easy, though," Lang added. "You're the enemy then, and they'll let you know it. Anyone can hit batting-practice pitching."

Glen caught the putdown but chose to ignore it. "I'll keep that in mind."

As game time approached, Holmes called his players together in the dugout and announced the lineups. Glen was disappointed and upset when his name wasn't called. He dropped onto the dugout bench and pounded his fist into his glove.

Thinking back through high school, Babe Ruth, and Little League, he couldn't remember ever being with a team and not starting.

The game against the Little Falls Mets got off to a rocky start. Utica found themselves down 2–0 after the first inning. The Mets, known for their great pitching throughout their system, seemed to have another winner on the mound this day. Through five innings, Utica failed to even get a hit.

Pacing up and down the dugout, Glen was going nuts. As the Sox batted in the sixth, he turned to Lang and said, "Is it always like this in here? Nobody's doing any cheering or anything?"

Lang laughed at him. "Hey, kid. This isn't high school ball anymore. No more rah-rah stuff. It's a job out there."

Glen was mad. "Well, it sure as hell doesn't look like anyone's working real hard. Maybe a little support and 'rah-rah stuff' wouldn't hurt!"

The lanky second baseman stood up and put

his finger on Glen's chest. "We don't need some smart-ass kid coming in here and telling us what we need. If I were you, I'd sit down and keep my mouth shut!"

Glen took a step closer to Lang and swatted his hand away from his chest. "Well, you're not me, and I don't need you to tell me how the game should be played."

The rest of the team started staring down at their two teammates and goading them on toward a fight.

Holmes overheard the exchange and ran down to step between his two players. "That's enough outta you two. Just sit down and shut up!"

Glen refused to make the first move. He remained toe to toe with Lang, staring into his angry eyes.

Holmes grabbed Lang's arm and yanked him backward. "Didn't you hear me? Sit down, both of you!"

When both players sunk to the bench, Holmes stood in front of Glen and scowled down at him. "Listen up, Mitchell. We're here to play ball. You cause trouble, you're out. Got it?"

Scrapper's competitive instincts drove him on. "Yeah, I got it. I came here to play baseball— *winning* baseball—not to sit on the bench!"

Holmes rubbed his chin and shook his head. "So, after five and a half innings of pro ball you think you've got it all figured out?" Holmes started to laugh. "I don't know how this team got along without you, Mitchell."

Fired up now, Scrapper didn't know when to quit. "It doesn't look like it's doing real well. . . ."

The rest of the Utica players waited for the explosion they knew was coming. Their manager was not one to be challenged. Glen continued before Holmes could unload on him. "I've sat here through five and a half innings, and it's been like sitting in a grave. What's wrong with a little chatter and support from everybody?"

Slowly, some of the other Utica players started to nod their heads and agree with Glen.

Holmes stepped forward, pushing his face within inches of Glen's. "Grab a bat, Mitchell. You're pinching for Samuels. Now!"

Glen brushed past his manager and confidently strode toward the bat rack. He found a batting helmet that fit and pulled out a thirty-three-ounce stick. He stood in the on-deck circle and carefully studied the motion of the Mets' pitcher, his emotions still surging from the confrontation.

Holmes turned to his pitching coach and chortled, "This'll show that hotshot what kinda pitching he's gonna be up against. Teach him about shooting off his mouth."

Utica's right fielder, Keith Jackson, stood in at the plate and worked the count to three and two. But Cory Snyder, the Mets' fireballing pitcher, fanned him on a called third strike.

Glen ran toward the batter's box and dug in a good foothold. He didn't bother to look down to the third-base coach for a sign. He knew he was on his own.

"I'd better make this good," Glen muttured under his breath. "Or I'll be sitting on the pines for a long, long time. Show me your stuff, ace!"

The Mets hurler rifled a fastball on the outside corner. Glen let it go. He knew there wasn't much he could do with it. The umpire bellowed out, "Striiiike one!"

A solitary voice cried out from the Sox dugout. "C'mon, Mitchell."

Glen couldn't tell if it was friend or foe. The fact that it was even yelled made him feel better.

The next pitch came blazing in high and inside. Glen knew it was a message pitch.

Reaching down for some dirt, Glen rubbed his hands together and tightened his grip on the bat.

The Mets' pitcher went into his windup and released the ball. It started out high and inside and then started breaking down and away. Glen smiled. This was his pitch.

He unleashed his swing and caught the pitch dead, solid, perfect. The ball took off like a bullet toward left field. It smashed against the cyclone fence and bounded along the warning track while the left fielder frantically chased after it. By the time the ball was returned to the infield, Glen stood on second base with a stand-up double.

The thousand or so Utica fans gathered in the stands started clapping and cheering. The public-address announcer came on, "That's the Sox' first hit of the ball game, and Glen Mitchell's first hit in his first at bat with the Sox. Let's give him a hand."

Glen kicked the bag at second and took a short lead. He refused to look over the dugout. Watching the pitcher intently, he heard a few more calls come out of the Utica dugout.

"Wayda go, Mitchell!"

"Looking good . . . looking good!"

Glen studied the Mets' hurler while he delivered a ball and a strike to the next batter. On the third pitch, Glen took off. Caught completely off guard, the Little Falls battery had no chance at catching glen. The throw came down to third well behind his headfirst slide. The umpire's hands spread out, signaling the call, "Safe!"

The calls and cheers from the dugout got louder. When Utica's shortstop took the next pitch and slapped it into left field for a single, Glen ran home with their first run and slapped high-fives with his teammates.

"Attaway, Mitchell!" "You're all right!" "Wayda hustle out there!"

Glen flipped his batting helmet off and flung it into the storage bin. He sat back down in the middle of the dugout and didn't say a word.

Utica's manager got up from his end seat and walked back down in front of Glen. He stood for a second without saying anything and then smiled. "Okay, kid. Nice work."

Glen stared up at him and let his adrenaline slowly subside before saying, "Thanks."

"Grab your glove and go in at second next inning, okay?"

Glen jumped to his feet with a huge smile on his face. "You betcha."

When Holmes walked the rest of the way down the dugout he stopped in front of Steve Lang and told him the bad news. "You're out the rest of the game, Lang. I'm letting Mitchell get his feet wet at second."

Lang nodded and angrily strode to the water cooler and then, when his manager turned away, walked up to Glen.

He pointed his finger at Scrapper and softly announced, "Don't think this is gonna be easy, Mitchell."

"I never thought it would be," said Scrapper.

"I'm not giving up without a fight," Lang said.

Glen stared back up at him. "You're on, man. Eat my dust."

FOUR

Roberto Ramirez stepped off the customized Trailways bus in Bend, Oregon and squinted in the bright sunshine. Still groggy from the time change and air travel, Roberto drew in a deep breath and let it out slowly. Having checked in with the Salem Dodgers only the day before, he was greeted with his first road trip before he was even settled.

"Hey, Ramirez, you forget something?" a voice called from the back of the bus.

Roberto glanced down and realized he'd left his travel bag behind. He bounced back up the two steps and said, "Sorry, Coach. I guess I'm still out of it."

The Salem manger laughed and patted Roberto on the shoulder. An older man, about sixty,

Alvin "Pops" Hanson loved baseball, and loved working with the new recruits. A veteran of forty years in baseball, he'd spent the last ten coaching rookie ball because of his talent for teaching.

"You're probably gonna be out of it for a while, son. It takes awhile to get in gear. But don't you worry. Everyone makes it through. I haven't lost anyone yet," Pops said.

"Glad to hear that," Roberto declared. "I hope I won't be the first."

The Dodgers checked into their motel rooms and then got right back on the bus to head to the ball park. Scheduled that night was a double-header against the Bend Angels.

The short bus ride from the motel took the team over the blue-green waters of the Deschutes River. Roberto couldn't believe how beautiful the setting was. The river ran through a stand of towering pine trees, and in the background were the majestic Cascade Mountains.

"Is all of Oregon this beautiful?" Roberto asked the player sitting next to him.

"Don't ask me. This is my first trip through the area myself," the teammate answered. "By the way, I'm not real good on names. I heard the coach introduce you yesterday, but I'm drawing blanks. . . ."

"Ramirez, Roberto Ramirez." Magic thought about his nickname but thought it best not to mention it.

"Slater, Chris. My friends back home always called me Deek, though."

"Deek? That's weird." A broad smile crossed Roberto's face.

"Well, back home growing up, I was a pretty fair hockey player. They slapped 'Deek' on me because of my moves around the goal."

"That's great. My friends called me Magic."

Deek laughed at Roberto. "You don't look like a basketball player. It must not be after Magic Johnson."

"Nope. They tagged me with Magic because of the trick pitches I could throw." Roberto felt self-conscious. "They thought I was pretty good."

Slater drove an elbow into his arm. "You must be if you're here."

Roberto nodded. "Yeah. I guess we all must have been pretty good in school to get this far. Say, what position do you play?"

"Center field."

"All right! One of my best friends on my high school team was the center fielder. . . . DT Green. In fact he just got drafted by the Red Sox and is playing in Elmira."

"Two players off the same team got drafted? That's amazing!"

"Hey, I can top that. Three players were. Our second baseman, Glen Mitchell, got picked by the White Sox and is playing in Utica."

Ryan Bondello, the Dodgers' third baseman, turned around from the seat in front of them.

"That's incredible! Three players off the same high school team? You guys must have had an awesome team."

Roberto beamed. "Won the state championship!"

Extending his hand, Ryan introduced himself.

"Glad to meet ya. How long have you guys been playing pro ball?" Roberto asked.

"We're both in our second year," Ryan answered. "We were kinda like you are now. We joined the team last year after getting drafted, so this is our first full year."

A frown crept onto Roberto's face. "So, playing in A ball for more than a year is kinda standard, or what?"

Ryan and Deek glanced at each other. They slowly started shaking their heads and Deek said, "Well, yeah, sort of. I guess. Most of the players have been here two, a couple of them, three years."

Roberto looked around the bus. He didn't remember seeing any old players on the team, now that he thought about it. "Can you guys tell me what I can expect in this league? I mean, was it a lot different than you thought it was gonna be when you started?"

Ryan laughed. "Yeah . . . I sure as heck think so. Deek here might not, since he's been pounding the cover off the ball ever since he got here. But, I've found it a lot tougher."

Deek slapped his empty Coke cup on Ryan's head. "Get lost, man. You do all right."

"You gotta remember," said Ryan, "we're looking at it from the hitter's side. I'll tell you the difference for me. In high school ball I'd face a good pitcher every four or five games maybe. Now the best of those four or five pitchers is throwing at us every night."

Deek added, "It can get kinda scary up there at the plate. Especially when you get some six-foot-six, two-hundred-and-forty-pound chucker who can throw the ball ninety-nine miles an hour but has no idea where it's going. If you know what I mean."

"I guess," whistled Roberto.

"Yeah. They draft any pitcher who can bring it in and just hope he learns some control." Ryan shook his head and poked Deek. "Remember that guy from Spokane last year? The guy who—"

"Say no more. I remember." Deek started laughing. "Check this out, Roberto. Spokane had this giant pitcher who threw so hard you couldn't hardly even see the ball. No kidding. Anyway, he uncorks one that starts rising. The catcher . . . well, he can't get his glove up fast enough and winds up taking it right in the face mask. Knocked him cold. After they carried him off the field, they had to fight to get the second-string catcher into the game. He didn't wanna go in."

Roberto flinched. "Sounds bad."

Ryan couldn't contain himself anymore.

"That's not even the good part. Deek was the next batter and—"

"Hey, give me a break. You wouldn't have been any better!" Deek claimed.

"Yeah. . . . Well, anyway, Deek's standing up at the plate next and he's inched so far out of the batter's box that the umpire keeps telling him he's got to stand up closer. Anyway, after the third warning, ol' Deeker here hands his bat to the umpire and tells him he can give it a try if he's so brave."

The entire front third of the bus who had been listening in on the story broke into laughter. As the team arrived at the Bend baseball field, Roberto felt more comfortable and at ease.

After pregame warm-ups, Pops Hanson yelled, "Roberto, come on down here and sit next to me in the dugout. We can go over the hitters and I can fill you in on a few things."

"Sure thing, Coach," Roberto said, happy to be getting the attention.

"I won't throw you into combat here for a few days. You've been on the road pretty much solid since you got here, so we'd better give you a chance to warm up properly, right?"

Roberto had never had trouble being ready to pitch, but accepted his coach's opinion. "Okay, Coach. But I think I'm ready to go if you need me. I'm used to throwing a lot."

"Well, we shouldn't have any need tonight. The whole staff is available. We were idle yesterday and got nine innings out of McGrain last game, so everyone else should be pretty well rested and ready to go."

Pops couldn't have anticipated the problems he wound up facing. His starting pitcher walked the first three batters he faced and never found the plate with one of the pitches. The first reliever lasted two innings before being taken out for a pinch hitter. Going into the bottom of the third, Salem was using their third hurler of the night.

The score remained tight, 4–3 Bend, for several more innings. When the Angels mounted a sixth-inning rally, Pops went to the bullpen once again. By the time the fire was out, two more Dodger firemen were out of the game.

With a great ninth-inning rally, Salem managed to pull out the win, 8–7. But not before two more relievers were needed to extinguish the last Bend threat. So after the first game of the doubleheader, the Dodgers had used six pitchers.

During the break between the two games, Roberto went out to the bullpen area and found one of the assistant coaches. "Say, do you mind if I make a few tosses? I haven't thrown for a couple of days and would like to loosen up a little."

Grabbing a catcher's mitt, Bob Marley, the

Dodgers' assistant manager, nodded. "Sure thing, kid. Let's see what you've got."

Roberto stretched and shook his arm to get the blood flowing. He grabbed a baseball and rubbed it in his hands. It felt good.

With an easy fluid motion, Roberto hurled a couple of pitches in to Marley. The oversized catcher's glove popped loudly with each impact.

"Hey, kid, take it easy. Don't throw too hard before you warm up a little," Marley yelled out.

Roberto shook his head. "I'm not. This is only three-quarters speed."

Marley stood up and turned toward the regular bullpen catcher, Jack Wiese. "Hey, Jack. Go run and get Pops. Tell him to get out here for a minute. I want him to see something."

Marley got back down in his crouch and signaled to Roberto. "Okay, Ramirez. Hum a few more in here."

Roberto's arm felt great. Happy to be throwing the ball again, his adrenaline was flowing and everything in the world seemed right. Each of his next four pitches increased in velocity.

Pops Hanson got out to the bullpen just in time to see and hear Marley's catcher's glove explode with each pitch. After watching ten or fifteen blistering fastballs, Pops called over to his new pitcher, "Hey, Ramirez. Does you arm feel good enough to try some curve balls?"

"No problem, Coach."

The next pitch came screaming in just like his last fastball. But just before it got to Marley, it broke down rapidly like an orange falling off a tabletop.

Winding up with the same motion each time, Roberto's next pitch was a big old roundhouse curve that swept from high and inside all the way across the plate to finish low and outside.

"*Whew*!" Marley exclaimed. "We've got ourselves a pitcher here, Pops!"

Hanson smiled and walked back toward the dugout.

The second game of the doubleheader, scheduled for just seven innings, started out uneventfully for both teams. After five innings, the game was a scoreless tie.

Hanson had Roberto by his side and talked strategy the whole game. "We have a pretty good book on some of these hitters now that we've seen them a few times. Notice how Martin out there works the outside corners on the guys we know like to pull the ball."

Roberto thought this was pretty basic stuff but nodded his agreement. "Yeah . . . that's good."

Hanson continued. "Then see how I've got the outfielders and infielders positioned? Knowing this guy wants to pull the ball and knowing we're gonna pitch him outside, we move the fielders into the alleys that he'll probably wind up hitting. Pretty easy, huh?"

Roberto smiled. "The whole team works together that way. Everybody knows what they should be doing, right?"

"You catch on quick, kid."

In the top of sixth, Salem scratched out a couple of hits and a stolen base and eked out a run to go ahead, 1–0. The Salem pitcher, Jim Martin, continued to breeze until the bottom of the seventh.

For some unknown reason, in the Angels' last at bat, Martin tightened up. After the first batter creamed a three-and-oh pitch up against the fence for a double, Martin could no longer find the strike zone. He walked the next two batters to load the bases.

"Damn!" Hanson cursed and walked out to the mound. After calling in the catcher to get his opinion, Pops took the ball from Martin and sent him to the showers. Pops pointed into the dugout and yelled out, "Ramirez, c'mon out!"

Roberto did a quick double take, but then grabbed his mitt and ran to the mound. They were joined by the catcher.

Pops handed him the ball. "Okay, kid. Do your best."

Roberto looked at him questioningly. He tugged on his cap and gulped out a reply. "Okay." The catcher went over the signs with Magic quickly.

Hanson returned to the dugout and his assistant, Bob Marley, came over to him. "What's the idea, Pops? A little baptism under fire?"

"Hey, I didn't want him to sit around a few days worrying about when he was gonna get a chance. This seemed like a good time to see how he reacts to pressure."

"You're the boss," Marley said.

"And you're the one who called me out to the bullpen to show me what the kid can do. I was impressed, same as you. Let's see if it's the same in a game!"

After his nine warm-up pitches, Roberto took a deep breath and looked around the infield. Runners stood at every base. The scoreboard out against the right-field wall showed the score was 1–0. Nobody was out.

Ryan Bondello, at third, yelled over to Roberto. "C'mon, Ramirez. You can do it. Plenty of help out here. Plenty of help!"

Magic nodded and tried to smile. He would work from the full windup since no one could steal. Leaning in and staring down at his catcher, Roberto got the sign.

Rearing back, Magic unleashed the full force of his whiplike arm and delivered his first professional pitch. Streaking across the inside corner of the plate, the ball burst in the catcher's glove and the umpire hollered out, "Strike one!"

Relieved, Roberto let out a deep sigh. Two more blazing fastballs, and he had recorded his first pro strikeout.

Hanson screamed out from the dugout, "Wayda go, Ramirez. Looking good out there!"

Roberto rubbed the baseball in his hands while the next batter came to the plate. He heard Deek Slater's voice from way out in center field. "Time for a little magic, Ramirez!"

Two more fastballs, and the count quickly jumped to oh-and-two on the next batter.

Marley elbowed Pops. "The kid looks sharp. Pressure or not, he's got a good setup and delivery. Doesn't hurry his body in front of his arm. Stays within himself and can still fire it. I like him!"

Hanson nodded. "Let's keep an eye on him. He's not outta this yet."

Roberto looked in for the sign from his catcher and shook him off. He waited for the signal he wanted and then nodded. With the same form and delivery, he threw another pitch toward the outside corner of the plate. The batter started to swing. He couldn't stop in time once he saw the ball starting to break. By the time the bat was crossing the plate, the ball was bouncing in the dirt.

"Strike three! You're outta there!" the umpire yelled.

With two outs, the Bend Angels sent their cleanup hitter to the plate. A mountain of a man, he seemed to fill the entire batter's box. Roberto couldn't believe how big he was.

Keeping the ball well away from him, Roberto missed the outside corner twice and fell behind two balls and no strikes. The batter's eyes seemed to light up, knowing that Roberto was going to have to throw strikes now.

Sucking up his breath, Magic dipped down

into his reserve of strength. He blazed the next pitch right down the middle of the plate. By the time the Bend hitter swung it was too late.

Slamming his bat down on the plate, he growled and stared out at Roberto.

Again Magic threw one right down the middle of the plate. But this time, it broke down and away from the batter's futile swing.

Seeing the confusion and anger in his face, Magic figured this batter would swing at an outside pitch now.

The pitch was a good one, but Roberto had misjudged the batter. He patiently watched the ball sail wide, and the count went to three and two.

The infield chatter increased. "C'mon, Ramirez. One more strike." "You can do it, Ramirez." "One time. One time!"

Magic felt the flow of adrenaline pulsing through his body. He took a deep breath and tried to focus his complete concentration on the catcher's target.

The Angels' behemoth batter dug in and growled out at the mound.

Winding up, Roberto directed every ounce of energy he could muster into the force behind his pitch. The ball came screaming in toward the plate . . . right down the middle.

The batter swung. The ball seemed destined to make fatal contact with the bat. But the tremendous velocity got it by the bat just in the nick of time.

"Strike three! You're outta here!"

The Salem players bounded into the air and ran toward their dugout. Winners 1–0!

Roberto accepted the congratulations and slaps on the back from his teammates as he walked back toward the dugout.

Pop Hanson turned to Bob Marley and smiled. He put his arm around his longtime assistant coach and nodded. "You know, I think we've got ourselves a pitcher. I think we've got ourselves a damn *good* pitcher!"

FIVE

Crumpling up the wrapper of his bag of fries and stuffing it into his empty Big Mac container, Dave Green took one last swig of his chocolate shake and stood up to leave. It was late and he headed for his new home—the Country Squire Inn.

He'd just been through his first game with the Sox. The effects of his travel and the week's excitement had caught up with him. By the time his head hit the pillow of his motel bed, he was fast asleep.

When he arrived at the ball park the next day, David was greeted by one of Elmira's coaches. "Hey, Green. Over here," yelled a deep, clear voice from the other end of the locker room.

David looked up to see a tall, heavyset man

in his early forties motioning toward him. Grabbing his hat and glove, David hurried across the noisy room.

Extending his hand in greeting, the older man introduced himself. "Hi. I'm Frank Brogan. How's it going?"

David cocked his head to one side and smiled. "Okay so far, I guess." He was unsure what he should say and how it would be taken.

"Well, I'm the batting instructor here in Elmira. I just wanted to introduce myself."

"Thanks. That sounds great." David gulped and looked around the room before asking in a soft voice, "When do I get to start playing?"

Brogan looked at his roster for the game. "You're batting fifth tonight . . . playing center field. The regular center fielder got called up to Double A and you're getting your chance to fill in. I'm here to make sure you're ready."

David lit up like a Christmas tree. "You bet I'm ready. That's terrific."

Brogan slapped him hard across the shoulders and laughed. "I like your enthusiasm, kid. You just keep that up no matter what happens, okay?"

"Sure thing, Coach."

"And one more thing. You can call me Brogie. You're gonna hear everyone else do it, so you might as well just start calling me that. I've been called just about everything else in the book, and I prefer it." Brogan's face broke into a wide grin. "That'll keep you from coming up with own wisecracking nickname for me."

David felt very at ease with his coach. "Okay, Brogie."

"Now, let's get out on the field and work some of the rust out of you."

"You got it," David yelled.

The Geneva Cubs had arrived in Elmira to start a three-game series with the Sox. Knowing the Cubs were in last place gave the Elmira team a feeling of confidence going into the game.

David watched the white-and-blue pinstriped Cubs' pregame drills as he paced up and down the dugout. The butterflies were flying in his stomach and he knew his palms were sweating as he tried to calm himself down for his big debut.

Johnny Sullivan, his manager, came over and tried to steady him. "Hey, Green, you ain't nervous, are ya?"

David could see the laughter in his coach's eyes. For some reason he immediately felt better. "Oh, no. Nothing like that. I'm just trying to break in a pair of shoes here, Coach. Thought walking up and down the dugout would help."

Sullivan squeezed David's arm. "You're right about that, kid. I go through three or four pair of shoes a year just walking up and down this concrete bunker. But listen, I don't want you to wear yourself out, so why don't you just park it for a while? The game's gonna start any minute now anyway."

"Okay," David replied.

When the Sox finally took the field to start the game, the small but enthusiastic crowd cheered wildly. And when David was introduced as the new starter in center field, he received a very warm round of applause, along with a few loud catcalls and jeers.

A heckler just beyond the center-field fence immediately caught David's attention.

"Hey, Green . . . hey, Green, you big bum . . . I hope you last longer than those idiots' last number-one pick. He's in Triple A now . . . he drives one of their tow trucks!"

David suppressed a laugh. He knew better than to let a fan get to him one way or another. "This is gonna be fun," he said out loud as the pitcher went into his windup.

The Cubs were retired in order with no plays for David out in center. As he came back into the dugout, he was still a little uptight, waiting for his first real action.

Elmira quickly went to work on the Cubbie pitcher and managed to load the bases with one out. As he threw his weighted practice bat back onto the on-deck circle, David strode to the plate for his first shot in the pros.

Green tamped down his red batting helmet and carefully dug himself a foothold in the batter's box. Taking a few practice swings, he settled into his stance and stared out at the pitcher. He saw a familiar sight in the Cubs' pitcher's eyes—fear—and felt he had him right where he wanted.

After the windup, the first pitch came hurtling toward the plate. David reared back and took a ferocious cut. He was surprised when he felt no contact.

"Strike one," yelled the umpire.

The rookie center fielder turned and looked in the catcher's glove as if to convince himself that he had missed the ball.

"C'mon, Green. Hang in there. Get a piece of it, get a piece of it," a voice from the dugout yelled.

"No problem," David said to himself.

The right-handed Geneva pitcher checked his sign and sailed a fastball that just missed the outside corner of the plate. The count evened at one and one.

"Good eye, good eye! Wayda watch 'em, kid!"

David felt good about the vocal support he was getting.

The next pitch, like the first, came steaming right down the middle of the plate. David cocked his bat and swung but, again, came away with nothing.

"Strike two!" went the call.

Frustrated, David slammed his bat on the plate and dug his cleats in deeper. More surprised than anything, he was determined to rip the next pitch he saw.

"Choke up a little, Green," Sullivan yelled. "Just get a piece of it."

David watched the Cubs' pitcher stalking around on the mound. He waited for him to take his spot on the rubber before settling down in the batter's box.

The crowd seemed to come alive after the second strike and was now rooting loudly for David. Their cheers pumped up his confidence once again.

"Okay, ace. Show me your stuff," David said to himself.

Working from the stretch to keep the runners close, the Geneva hurler started his delivery. The ball came floating in to the plate, and David's eyes grew bigger. Coiling at just the right moment, he whipped his bat around and through across the plate.

"Strriiikke three, you're outta here!" the umpire shouted.

Stunned, David turned and took the long, lonely walk back to the dugout. A few of his teammates patted him on the back as he walked by and plopped down hard on the dugout bench.

Sullivan walked down in front of him and clasped him behind his neck. "It happens, kid. Don't get down on yourself, okay?"

David tried a smile and a headshake but his heart wasn't in it. He couldn't figure out how he'd missed all three pitches.

The Sox managed another hit and scored two

runs, so when David took the field to start the second inning, Elmira was ahead 2–0.

As soon as he reached his position in center field, the heckler behind the fence went back to work on him.

"Looking good, *slugger*! You'll be carrying bats next game."

David wanted to spin around and confront his attacker but knew he shouldn't. He tried to focus all his attention on the batter up at the plate. Angry at himself for striking out and angry with the verbal abuse, David vowed to himself not to strike out again.

The Elmira team continued to cruise along with a 2–0 lead when they came up to hit in the bottom of the fourth. David was the lead-off batter. As he reached for his bat out of the rack, Frank Brogan wandered over and patted him on the back.

"Be relaxed up there, Green. Don't tighten up."

"Okay, Coach. I'll try."

"Take a couple of deep breaths and get in your rhythm. You can do it."

Nodding his head, David trotted out to the plate and took his stance.

"C'mon hotshot," someone in the stands yelled. "Let's start earning those bonus bucks!"

The grip on David's bat tightened a little.

Geneva's catcher looked up at David with a smile on his face and said, "What's the deal,

guy? You the new number-one pick or something? Is that why they're after ya?"

David just stared at the pitcher but shook his
head up and down.

"Hey, don't worry. I wish ya all the luck in the
world—against other teams," the catcher concluded.

The Cubs pitcher looked down at his opponent and took his sign from the catcher. He fired
two straight curve balls that just nicked the
outside corner of the plate for strikes. David
was caught looking at both of them.

"C'mon, Green. Be a hitter up there," a fan
yelled out.

"Do something with that big stick," another
hollered.

Frustrated, angry, and confused, David
stepped out of the box and wiped the nervous
perspiration from his forehead. He moved back
in and readied himself for the next pitch.

With the no-ball-and-two-strike count, the
rookie center fielder expected the pitcher to
waste a ball hoping to get a wild-swing third
strike. Instead, David watched as a pitch came
roaring down the middle of the plate.

A smooth but forceful swing produced nothing but air and another call from the umpire.
"Striiike three!"

Slamming his bat back in the rack, David
grabbed his hat and glove and walked to the far
end of the dugout and collapsed. His head sank
into his hands. He couldn't figure out what was

happening. David let out a deep breath and continued to stare in toward the infield.

The seventh inning came and resulted in another humbling strikeout for Elmira's newest player. As he walked back to he bench, dejected and upset, David got called to his manager's side.

"Hey, Green. You're pressing too hard. I'm gonna set you down for the rest of the game. Take some of the pressure off."

Stunned, David didn't know what to say. He had never been pulled from a game before in his life.

"Brogie, c'mon over here," Sullivan called over to his assistant coach. "I think we need to have a talk with our new recruit."

For the rest of the game, David sat in bewildered silence as he tried to overcome his horrible start. Occasionally, teammates would wander by and slap his knee or punch his side, offering their support as best they could.

His coaches refused to let him sink deeper into his private fog. They continued to talk about attitude and proper preparation. The game concluded with Elmira hanging on to a 4–3 win.

As the team filed out of the dugout and back toward the clubhouse, the former Rosemont star stood and shuffled his way out with the rest of the team.

Brogie called out to him as he approached the

door. "Hey, Green. Tomorrow we start working on hitting the scroogie."

"The what?" David said as he looked at him quizzically.

Brogie came up alongside him and put his arm around him. "Wouldn't you like to learn how to hit that pitch you missed six times today?"

"A scroogie?"

"Yeah, the ol' scewball. When a right-hander throws it to you lefties, it breaks down and away from you instead of down and in like a curve ball."

David shook his head. "They looked like regular old fastballs to me. When I—"

"They're supposed to, kid. Why do you think you got fooled so bad?"

David couldn't answer.

"You swung at pitches you couldn't hit with a shovel. All of them broke down into the dirt as they went by you."

David tried to reconstruct his at bats in his mind. The pitches seemed good to him every time he replayed them mentally. "I sure thought they were strikes."

"Hey. Don't worry about it. Valenzuela's made millions getting hitters to swing at those crummy pitches. You're no different than anyone else."

"I didn't see anyone else strike out three times today."

Brogie laughed. "That's because they've all

had me as a batting instructor. You just wait. I'm gonna teach you how to lay off those pitches."

"How?"

"The key is picking up the rotation of the ball as soon as it leaves the pitcher's hand. Once you can identify the pitch, then you can do something with it. Even if it's just letting it go by. That's all stuff you have to learn, and we'll work on that tomorrow."

"Thanks, Coach."

Brogie smiled and walked away, calling over his shoulder, "Ten sharp, the batter's cage. Be there."

SIX

The Utica White Sox were on a roll. So was Scraps Mitchell. Since his stormy introduction to the team, the former Rosemont Rocket had become the unquestioned leader on the field. The effects of his play and the change in attitude of the rest of the team had resulted in a nine-game winning streak.

From a position buried in the cellar of the New York–Penn league, the White Sox had edged their way ahead of two teams and stood alone in third place. After their dismal start, the players were now talking up the chance of having a winning season, maybe even the pennant.

Celebrating their latest win in the clubhouse after the game, Glen was laughing and snapping towels at anyone who happened to walk by. He caught himself just in time as his manager walked into range.

"Oops . . . Sorry, Coach," Glen said, folding up his towel and tossing it onto the bench.

Ted Holmes, the Utica manager, didn't bat an eye. He was so happy with the new, improved atmosphere around his team that Glen had become one of his favorites.

"The way you're hitting, Mitchell, I can't believe you missed." Changing his voice to a grumble, he added, "But it's a good thing you did!"

Glen continued getting dressed as he talked. "Say, Coach, when's our first road trip, anyhow?"

Holmes looked at his watch, a habit he had developed that gave him extra time to think before he answered questions. "Funny you should mention that, Mitchell. Be sure and pack your bag tonight. We're leaving tomorrow for twelve days."

"All right! Where're we going?"

"Don't ask where we're going, ask where we're not going. It's a shorter list."

Glen thought about his friend David. "Elmira?"

Holmes started to walk away as he said, "First stop. Tomorrow night."

Glen hadn't expected to get a chance at seeing Dave Green until later in the season. Now he was going to play against him.

* * *

Glen arrived at the ball park early the next morning, suitcase and equipment bag in hand, anxious for his first road trip. Being the first one there, he paced up and down in the parking lot, waiting for his other teammates and the bus to arrive.

He was surprised when a beat-up old Greyhound, custom painted an awful shade of green, pulled up. A gray-haired old man, sixtyish, stumbled out the front door.

"Morning," he drawled when he spotted Glen. "You're early, ain't ya?"

Glen sauntered over to the driver. "I thought the coach said to be here by seven."

Breaking into a cackling laugh, the old man said, "He's been telling you rookies that for years . . . just to make sure that everyone gets here by nine."

"What a rip! I could've slept late."

"Hey, it might've been worse—like the time the bus broke down, leaving the whole team to wait in the rain. And, they still had to play at the other end, too."

"I sure would've been mad." He stuck out his hand. "By the way, my name is Glen Mitchell, but my friends call me Scrapper. I play second base."

The old man shook his hand. "Franklin, Hanford T. But my friends—and my enemies I guess—all call me 'Whiplash'—on account of my careful drivin'."

Glen looked at the beat-up side of the bus. "There isn't any other reason is there?"

"Well, now . . . I have had a scrape or two in my day, if that's what ya mean. Never have lost a passenger, though." The old-timer reached in his back pocket and pulled out a package of chewing tobacco. "Wanta plug?"

Glen scratched his head, then looked at Whiplash's brown teeth, what were left of them, and shook his head. "Nah . . . you go ahead. I don't chew."

"And it's a damn good thing you don't. Disgusting habit when you git right down to it." He shook his head and took a big bite out of the dark brown plug.

Glen moved back a few steps so that he'd be out of spitting range. "You seem to know a lot about the team. What else can you tell me beside schedules?"

Whiplash spat at the curb. "Well, the rest of the boys'll probably be coming up with some good jokes for you—you being the new guy and all. It's your friends you have to watch out for."

Glen and Whiplash continued to talk until the rest of the team started showing up. When everyone was finally there and the baggage was loaded, the long bus ride got under way. As the newest member of the team, Glen had to sit up front next to the manager.

Ted Holmes plopped down in the seat next to Glen and folded open his copy of the *Sporting News*. As the bus rolled through beautiful upstate New York, Glen listened to his manager grunting and chuckling as he read the paper.

"What's so interesting in there, Coach?"

Holmes lifted one eye and shifted it toward Glen without moving his head. "What's the matter with you, boy? Don't you read the *Sporting News*?"

"Well, yeah, I've read it before. What's the big deal?"

Holmes folded the paper up and dropped it on his lap. "When you've been around as long as I have, seen as many players as I have, you kinda want to know how they're doing after they leave Utica. You know what I mean?"

"Oh, yeah. Sure. I understand now. The *Sporting News* has all the stats for minor-league players . . ."

"Right! Now, take my first baseman last year . . . Reilly. He's up with Birmingham in Double A now. He's batting three twenty-two and hammered out ten home runs already. Not bad, huh?"

"Gee, that's great. Do you think he's gonna get moved up again soon?"

Holmes rubbed his forehead. "Never can tell, kid. There's a lot of factors involved."

Glen looked twice at his manager. "Whaddaya mean?"

"Pro ball is a business. Reilly's hitting great and he's fast on the bag. But the big club is pretty well set at first right now. So they're not looking to bring him up any time soon. The

Triple A team . . . Vancouver . . . has a guy batting three forty, with a gold glove in the field."

"That's great!"

"Yeah, but not for Reilly. Where's he gonna go? Are they gonna ask him to learn a new position? Or just let him sit a couple of years playing Double A until something breaks—or maybe trade him?"

Glen shrugged his shoulders. "What do you think?"

"First off, let me tell you, the parent club never wants to get rid of a good prospect unless they're getting something concrete in the deal. Like a Wade Boggs trade for two other all-stars and two minor-league players to be named later. That kinda thing."

"Gotcha." Glen nodded.

Holmes folded his arms and leaned back. "But those deals don't come along too often. So my guess is they'll keep him buried in Birmingham as an insurance policy for the two guys above him. Unless he becomes such a hot property that he has to be moved."

"Well, that's kinda lousy for Reilly, isn't it?"

"Real lousy. But like I just said, kid, it's a business. The players are the commodity you're dealing with, and they have to be handled without emotion or sentiment."

"So you're saying, it's not just how good you are that determines your fate in pro ball."

"Exactly. That's why you'll find most every

guy in the back of the bus there checking the stats. They're looking to see how the people up and down the line from them are doing. You've got to have one eye on your goal in front of you and one eye on the competition coming up from behind. If they don't keep up, well, they won't be around long, is my guess."

Glen sank down in his seat. He tried to remember who was playing second base for the Chicago White Sox.

Holmes kept right on talking. "Best position to be is a catcher. There's just flat-out always a shortage of good catchers. Parents don't want their little Bobby hunched down behind the plate with all the gear on, wearing out his knees. They want him to be a pitcher or a shortstop. Glamorous and exciting positions."

"How about second base?" Glen laughed.

Holmes nodded his head. "Good spot for little Bobby. Doesn't have to have as strong an arm. Doesn't have to be a great hitter. Good fielder who doesn't make mistakes will always get to play second. It's when you find one that can hit . . . now then you've really got something!"

Holmes took a long stare at Glen.

Scrapper tried to divert his attention. "What about center fielders?"

"The quickest ticket to the majors. A fleet-footed, sure-handed, power-hitting center fielder. Show me one and I'll show you a star!"

Glen smiled. "You're gonna see one tonight, Coach."

* * *

By midafternoon, Utica's dark green bus rolled across the Chemung River and entered the quiet town of Elmira. Making its way directly to the ball park, the bus screeched to a stop in the parking lot. The players slowly unfolded their arms and legs and stretched and staggered out into the afternoon sunshine.

Glen barely had time for his eyes to adjust to the brightness when he heard a familiar voice call out from the field.

"Hey, Scrapman!"

The entire Utica team turned to find the source of the voice.

Glen spotted his buddy, David Green, playing catch in the grass outfield of the ball park. Running toward the fence, he waved and yelled out, "DT. My man. How the hell are ya?"

When they reached each other they quickly fell back into their old team greeting of smashing forearms, and then hugged each other.

"Geez, it's good to see ya, Mitchell." David's voice quivered for a minute. "I've really missed you!"

"I've missed you, too, man. How's it going?"

David just shook his head and threw off a quick reply. "Okay. How're you doing?"

Glen could tell things weren't right with his friend. Always filled with confidence and brimming with enthusiasm, David was obviously not himself. But Glen wanted to share his good news with his best friend. "Fantastic. The team's been winning, everything's been going great!"

David flashed his winning smile. "That's outta sight. You must be pumped."

"Yeah. We've won nine in a row now. We're on a roll!" Glen poked his buddy in the chest. "Now, the truth. What's going on here with you?"

David pushed his hat back on his head. "It's been tough, Scrapper. Real tough. My hitting's down. Right-handers not so bad, but left-handers have been getting to me. I don't know what's wrong."

"Doesn't sound like the DT I know."

"Yeah, well it hasn't been." David was embarrassed to say it. "I haven't even hit a home run here."

"What!" Glen was shocked.

"I'm only hitting about one fifty. I haven't had enough contact with the ball to hit one out. I'm just lucky the coach has been sticking with me at all."

Glen whistled in shock. "I can't believe it." He was too self-conscious to tell David that he was batting .325.

David looked down at the grass and nervously kicked at a puff ball. "It's just so different from high school. Every night we've faced some phenom who throws BBs."

"But you used to eat fastballs for snacks. I haven't seen anybody that good—"

"Hey, it's the junk they throw in between that's got me screwed up." Frustrated, David threw his glove up in the air and caught it. "I don't know. I must be doing something wrong."

Glen heard his manager call and waved back up toward the bus. "Look, guy, I've got to get going here. Let's get together tonight after the game and eat something and talk. You must know the best burger place in town by now."

David laughed. "Well, yeah, I do know a pretty good spot."

"Well, at least you haven't forgotten everything." Glen pushed David in the chest and flipped his hat off the back of his head. "Hey, stay loose tonight. It'll be like old times—only I'll be watching your rockets from the infield instead of the dugout."

David slapped his buddy on the back of the shoulder. "Thanks, pal. Later, man."

"No problem." Glen started to walk toward his bus. "Hey, but one other thing . . ."

"Yeah?"

"Don't get mad when we beat you tonight, all right?"

David waved him off. "In your dreams, Mitchell."

When he got back up by his teammates, Glen was hammered with questions and insults.

"*Scrapman?* What the heck is all that?" they teased.

Glen grabbed his bag and tried to ignore them.

Whiplash pulled down the flap of the luggage compartment and set the record straight. "Now, gentlemen, didn't y'all know that this here man's nickname was Scrapper? You've been playing ball with him all this time, an' me, I just met him today and knew that. What's wrong with you guys?"

"*Hey*, Scrapper! I like the sound of that. Great name. Great, great name." The comments flew around.

As the team made their way toward the locker room, everyone joined in the fun of teasing Glen. Everyone except Steve Lang.

As the team entered the dark interior of the building, Lang thought to himself, *Enjoy it now, Scrapper! I'm not through with you yet.*

SEVEN

The Elmira team finished their pregame warm-ups and returned to the dugout. The game with Utica was about to begin and David felt an unfamiliar attack of nerves flair up. He hadn't felt like this since his first game in high school. But since his slow start with Elmira, a lot of his old cocky confidence was missing. For the first time in his life, David was struggling with baseball.

He was relieved when the coach signaled for the team to take the field. When he reached his position and turned around to face the infield, he was surprised to see his old friend, Glen Mitchell, leading off the White Sox.

Elmira started their usual chatter out in the field, but David was faced with an unusual feeling. "Geez, I can't yell anything crummy about Scrap," he mumbled to himself. But then, with a shrug, he changed his mind. "Ah, what the heck."

At the top of his lungs, he screamed, "Batter ain't nothing! Hum it by him, hum it by him!"

David thought he saw Glen smile up at the plate.

Elmira's pitcher started out with a fastball over the outside corner of the plate. He quickly learned that wasn't the pitch.

Glen reached out over the plate and smacked the ball into center field for a clean single. David loped in and scooped up the grounder. With a relaxed fluid motion, he pretended he was throwing to second, but instead, whirled and rifled the ball back to first, trying to fool his old teammate.

Glen stumbled for a split second but then righted himself and slid back into first safely. He stood up, shook the dirt off himself, and then turned out to face center field. He doffed his cap toward his high school buddy.

David smiled.

Utica wasted no time in capitalizing on Scrapper's hit. The next batter laid down a sacrifice bunt, advancing Glen to second. The next batter delivered with the man in scoring position, rapping a single into right field. As David ran off the field, the Red Sox were behind the White Sox, 1–0.

"Nice try, Green," his manager said as David

hopped down into the dugout. "Smart play . . . you almost got him."

"I knew he was gonna be aggressive making the turn, and I thought it might work." David chuckled. "I should have known he'd find a way back."

Johnny Sullivan stared at his young rookie. "You know that guy already?"

"Already?" David laughed. "I've known him for years, Coach. That's Glen Mitchell! We played high school ball together."

Sullivan looked out toward the field. "So that's the guy, huh. I've heard he's been tearing up the league since he started a couple of weeks ago."

David felt sheepish thinking about his own miserable start. "Yeah, he's the best."

Sullivan grabbed David by the collar with both hands. He backed him up against the wall of the dugout. "Listen to me, kid. Every report I've ever gotten on you said you were the driving force on that team. I been patient with you long enough. It's time to get your head outta the ground and start producing. Do I make myself clear?"

The whole dugout fell silent. Johnny Sullivan was usually a very quiet, good-natured manager. The sudden outburst caught everyone by surprise.

"Yes, sir," was all David could stutter out. He sank down on the bench and tried to melt into the woodwork.

Having been dropped to seventh in the batting order, David knew he probably wouldn't bat in the first inning. After the tongue-lashing from his coach, he hoped he could get back on the field as soon as possible.

Elmira was retired quietly in their half of the first, and Utica went down quickly in the top of the second. The fans, enjoying the warm summer evening, settled in for a defensive battle.

After the first Elmira batter was retired in the bottom of the second, Jose Olivares singled. David moved into the on-deck circle and anxiously waited his turn. He watched Glen, pacing around at second, barking out orders to his teammates, seemingly in complete command. It didn't seem that his old Rosemont teammate had missed a beat since turning pro.

When the next Sox hitter grounded out, moving Olivares to second, David walked to the plate. "Okay, Green. It's time," he told himself.

Digging in with his cleats, David focused his eyes on the pitcher standing out on the mound. He didn't want to chance looking at Glen, fearing that his concentration would be broken.

The first pitch came zipping in and David made a powerful cut at it. Catching it on the top of his bat, he lifted a high foul ball back behind the plate up in the stands.

He thought he heard a familiar voice calling out from the infield. "Two more. Two more. This guy's not so tough!"

David's imposing size made every pitcher

work him carefully. The next three pitches were well outside and away from his potential power.

David checked for the sign with his third-base coach. With two out, he expected nothing but the hit-away sign, and that's what he got.

Utica's right-handed pitcher came back in with a fastball moving inside. David again coiled up and unleashed a ferocious cut. But again his contact was weak and the ball dribbled foul, bouncing down to the first-base coach.

"C'mon, Green," Sullivan yelled from the dugout. Get a hold of something, will ya?"

Glancing toward his manager, David saw him standing next to his batting coach, Frank Brogan. His manager was scowling, but Brogie was flashing him a thumbs-up signal and a wink.

The next pitch was a slow curve. David eyed it carefully. It was the kind of ball he used to take and drive out of the park without a second thought. But now he hesitated and stood as it dipped by him. The umpire looked down at his indicator and motioned toward first.

"Ball four, take your base!"

Trotting down to first, David felt a mixture of relief and disappointment. He hadn't hurt his team by going out, but he hadn't helped himself by getting a hit.

He heard Brogie calling from the dugout. "Good eye, Green. That's the way to wait for 'em."

David knew it was a hollow endorsement.

Edging off the bag as the pitcher toed the

rubber, David glanced over toward Glen. Their eyes met and a smile danced across each boy's face.

When the count went to one ball and two strikes on the next Elmira hitter, David was surprised to get a signal from the third-base coach to steal. As the next pitch was released, he and Olivares both broke from their bags. Caught off guard, Utica was a victim of the double steal.

Standing on second, David brushed the dirt off his white uniform and straightened his batting helmet. Glen walked by and kicked the bag.

"Stand up straight," Utica's second baseman whispered as he moved away from the base.

"Huh?" David stuttered.

Walking back toward his position with his head down, Glen murmured in a low voice, "You're all crouched up at the plate. Stand up straighter."

David tried to think back to his stance during his last at bat. He didn't think he was doing anything differently, but he decided to try next time. He took his lead off the bag.

Elmira's next hitter, Juan Sambriello, hit a soft liner over the shortstop's head. Racing around third, David never even looked for the sign from his third-base coach. With a final burst of speed, he dove headfirst, his outstretched hand just nipping home before the throw. His daring run staked Elmira to a 2–1 lead.

Coach Sullivan greeted David as he stepped down into the dugout. "Good hustle, Green."

"Thanks, Coach."

The next two innings produced no scoring. The only real threat came when Glen slammed a long drive into the gap between left and center. Elmira's left fielder, Jason Thomas, made a spectacular grab up against the fence to rob Scrapper of a potential home run. When David approached the plate in the bottom of the fifth, the score was still 2–1 Elmira.

As he stepped up to the batter's box, David recalled his friend's words of advice: "Stand up straight."

When he assumed his usual position at the plate, David made a conscious effort to stand straight. Taking a few practice swings, he noticed that his swing was much more fluid.

Feels good, the former Rosemont slugger said to himself.

Utica's pitcher started David out the same as the first at bat: a fastball on the outside corner. But this time, he quickly flashed his bat around and slammed a solid line drive toward the hole between first and second. Before he could take his first step out of the batter's box, David saw the angle between his drive and his friend, Scrapper, and knew he was doomed.

"Damn!" he yelled as he flung his bat down.

But then he noticed something. Nobody else would have been able to pick it up, it was so subtle. It was four years of playing together that gave David more insight than the others involved.

Glen hadn't reacted with the crack of the bat. A split second went by before he made his move. By the time he took two steps and leaped into the air, the ball just kissed off the edge of Glen's glove. David was on with a clean single to right.

"Attaway to hit 'em, Green. Better! Much better!" Sullivan hollered out.

With a quick nod to his skipper, David turned back toward the field of play and stole a glance at Glen. The White Sox second baseman went back into his crouch at second and ignored his old high school buddy.

"C'mon, men. Let's get these guys. Lucky hit, lucky hit!" Glen shouted.

Any doubts about favoritism were quickly erased. Elmira's very next batter bounced a ball toward shortstop. The quick flip to second forced David coming down from first. Glen took the toss, spun, and fired a bullet to first, directly at his friend's head. Dodging the relay, David turned and headed back for the dugout. The throw to first was perfect and just in time for the double play. Elmira was retired quietly to end the fifth.

The top of the seventh inning found Glen Mitchell leading off the inning again. The score had been 2–1 since the second. Enjoying the fast pace of the game, the crowd was vocal in their support for their home team, the Red Sox. A loud boo greeted Glen as he approached the plate.

David bounced up and down on his toes while standing out in center field. He was keeping his legs loose, ready to run when necessary, and also secretly cheering for his buddy to do well.

"C'mon, Scrapper. Show 'em whatcha can do!" he whispered.

When Elmira's pitcher wound up and threw, Scrapper was ready. He laced a single in the hole between short and third.

Jason Thomas jogged in to retrieve the ball and throw it back to second. Seeing an opening, Glen rounded first on the dead run and raced toward second. Thomas caught on too late and hustled to get to the ball, then zipped the throw to second. Glen was already there.

Utica's bench erupted in cheers.

"Wayda run, Mitchell!"

"Beautiful . . . beautiful!"

"That's a start. Let's get 'em now!"

David simply smiled out in center field. He'd seen it all before.

Fired up now, the White Sox rallied for three runs and took a 4–2 lead into the seventh-inning stretch.

As David ran off the field, he waited for the familiar blast from the organist. Or, as Jeff Lang had explained to him one night, a tape recording of the organist playing that old ball-park favorite, "Take Me Out to the Ball Game!"

Utica's pitcher seemed inspired by the rally, also. He set the Red Sox down in order in the seventh and eighth innings and went to the mound in the ninth, still protecting that 4–2 advantage.

When the first Elmira batter, their cleanup hitter, struck out, a gloom descended over the team's dugout. It seemed their best chance was now gone.

But a glimmer of hope sparked when Olivares walked, and then Thomas singled. With one out, runners on first and second, David Green strode to the plate.

Utica's manager called time and walked out to the mound to talk to his pitcher. Frank Brogan took the opportunity and called David back over.

Worried that he was being replaced, David hung his head as he walked back toward the dugout. Brogie quickly cleared the air.

"Hey, Green. Heads up. I'm not yanking ya."

David immediately brightened. "Great!"

"I just wanted to warn you about what to expect. He's consistently tried to pitch you away, so don't fight it. Don't try to pull the ball."

David nodded.

"You've got enough strength you don't need to try and overpower the ball. Just go with the pitch."

The conference out on the mound ended, and Elmira's rookie center fielder returned to the plate. He carefully positioned himself in the box and worked hard at setting himself up properly at the plate.

A familiar voice called out from second to the Utica pitcher. "Be careful with this guy . . . be careful!"

David took a practice swing and then smiled.

The first pitch came bearing down on him. It was obviously on the outside edge of the strike zone again. But this time, David was ready. A smooth, almost effortless swing produced a result the Elmira fans had never seen. Glen Mitchell hung his head and got set to run off the field. He had seen it many times before.

The ball jumped off David's bat and headed for straightaway center field. As he headed for first, DT knew he'd be running around the field.

The ball was still sailing when it cleared the bleachers and disappeared across a road behind the park. The three-run blast, David's first as a professional, gave Elmira a stirring 5–4 victory and snapped Utica's nine-game winning streak.

As he rounded third base, he saw the crowd of his cheering teammates gathered at home. When he ran across the plate, he absorbed the backslaps and cheers with a big grin. David felt relieved and very happy.

Later he dressed and prepared to meet his old buddy after the game. *It's going to be like old times after a Rocket win*, David thought. *Too bad Magic can't be with us.*

EIGHT

After several sparkling outings as a relief pitcher, Magic Ramirez was getting the first start of his professional career. He had thrown a total of twelve innings in his previous four appearances and had managed an eye-popping .083 ERA and three saves. He'd also struck out sixteen batters. The Dodger coaching staff thought he was ready to move into the starting rotation.

Roberto Ramirez loosened up his arm in the Dodgers' bullpen. He stopped to stare up at the blue skies and high white clouds over Salem, Oregon when he heard Pops Hanson. "How goes it, Ramirez?"

Magic looked around for the source of the

voice and then waved an okay signal at him. "Terrific. The arm feels just great."

"Glad to hear it, kid. C'mon over here for a minute."

Pulling out a crumpled piece of paper, Hanson studied it carefully, then pointed out the highlights to his young pitcher.

"Here's tonight's batting lineup for Spokane. You probably went over the whole team last night with Lumpy, right?"

Magic nodded his head. Lumpy was Salem's catcher. A happy-go-lucky attitude masked an excellent baseball mind and a fierce competitor. The two of them had spent the better part of three hours in Lumpy's room going over each hitter on Spokane's team. Lumpy got his nickname from being short and slightly overweight.

Hanson's finger centered on two players. "These guys, Pagliano and Ho, don't challenge them. So far this year they've answered every challenge."

"Yeah. Lumpy was telling me they're burning up the league right now. Pagliano's hit thirteen dingers already, and Ho's batting four-oh-seven. I figured they must be the ones to stop. No one else on the team seems like they're doing much."

Hanson patted Ramirez on the shoulder. "Good, you've got that figured. Now listen to me. I want you to be relaxed out there and just pitch."

"Sure. No problem."

"Don't be trying to throw everything by these guys, either. Pace yourself. I'd like to see you go seven innings tonight."

Roberto looked surprised. Whenever he took the mound he expected to go all the way. "This is a nine-inning game, isn't it?"

Pops tugged the brim of Roberto's cap down over his eyes. "Just give me seven good innings . . . we've got a decent bullpen, you know."

Roberto shrugged. "At least seven."

When Hanson left, Roberto returned to the rubber and continued to warm up. The evening was pleasantly warm. Attendance looked like it was going to be good. Everything seemed in place to Roberto. He stopped for a minute and thought back to his old high school buddies again. *I wonder how Scrapper and DT are doing right now . . . .*

The Salem public-address announcer came on with a list of messages, signaling the start of the game. Roberto took one more pitch and then trotted to the dugout to wait for the introduction.

The crackle and hum of the speaker system finally blared out, "And now, ladies and gentlemen, your Salem Dodgers!"

A warm round of applause greeted the players as they took the field. It was the first game back after a long road trip, and the team felt great hearing some encouragement for a change.

Roberto strutted out to the mound, head high, chest out, happy to be starting off.

The first Spokane batter stepped in at the plate. Roberto tossed the rosin bag down behind the mound and stared in for the sign. Lumpy flashed one finger, calling for a fastball, and Magic nodded. The Spokane batter never knew what went by him—three times.

"You're out!" The batter walked off.

Roberto breezed through the next batter, also. Six pitches. Six strikes. Two outs. The crowd started buzzing in amazement.

"Who is that out on the mound?" "That boy can throw!" "Isn't that L.A.'s first-round draft pick this year, you know, the kid from Illinois?"

As the game progressed, it wasn't long before everyone in the stands knew his name. The public-address announcer kept saying, "Another strikeout for Roberto Ramirez!"

After four innings, Magic had struck out nine batters and held the Padres hitless.

With the Dodgers batting in the bottom of the fourth, Pops Hanson came and sat by Roberto's side. "Nice work, kid. How's the arm holding up? You're throwing pretty hard out there."

Magic flashed him a toothy smile. "The arm feels brand new, Coach. The ball's just popping for me tonight!"

Hanson laughed. "Keep it up. But remember, seven innings."

The Dodgers managed a rally in their half of the fourth. Three hits and a couple of walks produced three runs and staked Roberto to a comfortable lead.

The length of the Dodgers' turn at the plate, coupled with the cooling evening temperature, started to wear him down. When he finished his warm-up tosses he noticed a little tightness in his arm.

The first batter for the Padres in the fifth was Danny Ho. Roberto remembered the story about Spokane's leading hitter—in fact, the Northwest League's leading hitter.

Danny was the first player in minor-league ball to come out of the successful baseball program in Taiwan. Ho had led his Taiwan team to the Little League World Series back in 1980. His .370 average in the championship game gave his team the world championship. Now he was back in the United States making his way in professional ball.

Roberto eyed him carefully. He could see that Ho was confident and knowledgeable as he stood in at the plate. Relaxed, well balanced, he kept his eye trained on the pitcher.

Lumpy flashed two fingers, calling for a curve ball. Roberto nodded and rifled a beauty right at Ho. Without blinking an eye, the batter stood in position and waited for the ball to break down and away from him. When it did, his short, compact stroke laced the ball into center field for a single. Roberto's no-hitter was gone.

When the ball came back to him from the outfield, Magic looked over at the runner on first. Roberto had to tip his hat to Ho out of respect. The Taiwanese batter had hit one of his best pitches.

That guy is really good, Magic thought as he rubbed up the baseball. *What's it gonna be like if I ever make it to the majors?*

The brief moment of self-doubt ended when he retired the next three Padres in order, two more by strikeouts. After five complete innings, Salem still led 3–0.

Lumpy came and sat down next to Roberto between innings. He kept his catcher's gear on since he wasn't scheduled to hit unless the Dodgers had a big rally. He whistled through his teeth as he peered around the dugout.

"He hit a good pitch, Ramirez. Not much ya can do about something like that. No big deal. We're still cruisin'."

"No problem," agreed Roberto. "We'll get 'im next time."

The sun finally completed its descent, and the bright artificial lights were now the only illumination for the field. The temperature quickly dropped ten more degrees and the warm eighty-degree temperature at game time was now replaced by sixty-degree coolness. Roberto was surprised by the dramatic change.

"This sure isn't like Illinois," he told his catcher as they took the field to start the sixth.

Lumpy laughed. "Or Little Rock, my hometown. It's probably still ninety there."

"That'd be tough."

"The pitchers back home loved it. They said they had no trouble keeping loose, and their curve ball seemed to break better to 'em there."

Both players laughed and went out to their positions.

Roberto struck out two more batters in the sixth and one in the seventh, bringing his total for the game to fourteen. As he walked toward the dugout at end of the inning, the crowd gave him a huge ovation.

While Salem was tacking on two more runs in their half of the seventh, Pops Hanson walked over to his catcher. "How's his arm, Lumpy?"

"Seems great, Coach."

"He hasn't lost any speed yet?"

Lumpy shook his glove hand. "Heck, no! Those last two fastballs really popped. I'm not kidding ya, Coach, I think he's picked up a notch or two the last two innings."

Hanson cocked his head to one side. "Son of a gun . . ."

With a commanding 5–0 lead, Roberto ran out to the mound in the eighth, convinced his first win was only six outs away. But the P.A. announcer's update made him think of something else.

"Salem's Roberto Ramirez is just three strike-outs short of the Northwest League record for a nine-inning game. Let's show our support for him with a big hand."

The crowd rose to their feet and started clapping. Now, with every pitch, they groaned or cheered depending on the call.

Roberto started to feel some nervous perspiration on his forehead as he faced the last batter in the eighth. The first two batters had grounded out and the crowd was starting to give up on their hopes for a record.

Running the count to two balls and two strikes on the batter, Roberto reached down for something a little extra and blazed a fastball down the middle. The Padre's swing was way too late and the announcer cried out, "That's *fifteen!*"

Pops Hanson watched his young hurler walk in from the mound. He was concerned that Roberto was getting caught up in something he shouldn't. He motioned him to his side.

"Sit down here a minute, Ramirez. I wanna talk to ya."

Mopping his brow with his sleeve, Roberto plopped down next to him. "What's up, Coach?"

"Listen, kid. It looked like you were gonna bust a gasket on that last pitch. I don't want ya to get carried away here. Don't let the crowd dictate how you throw. Stay within yourself . . . you follow?"

"Yeah, sure, Coach. I'm okay . . . really."

"I want you to stay okay. That's my point. Don't go throwing your arm out trying for some fool record. This is your first game in your first year of pro ball. Play your cards right and you might have a career in baseball."

Roberto felt the full impact of his words. ". . . a *career* in baseball." *If that wasn't a vote of confidence I don't know what is,* he thought.

When Pops walked away, Lumpy quickly came to his battery mate's side. "What was all that about?"

Roberto smiled. "A little friendly advice, that's all."

Lumpy stood up and lightly tapped Roberto's shoulder. "The way you're throwing, just do what you do, man."

When the Dodgers recorded their third out, Roberto hopped up and started to trot to the mound. Pops caught him one more time with a steely eye. "Keep it smooth, Ramirez."

The first batter up for Spokane was Danny Ho. Roberto thought back to his base hit that broke up the no-hitter, the only hit of the game for the Padres. *No curve this time,* he decided as he looked for the sign.

Lumpy was on the same wavelength. He put down one finger and moved his glove to the outside corner of the plate.

Roberto wound up and delivered right on target. But Ho's bat once again knew where the target was and beat the ball there. He ripped another single into center field.

"What does it take to get this guy out?" Roberto said out loud as he reached for the rosin bag. He saw Pops Hanson get up and head out of the dugout.

Lumpy pulled off his mask and met his pitcher and manager on the mound. Pops's first question was directed to him. "Is it time?"

Roberto looked confused. He was about to learn that Lumpy often was the one to make the call on a relief pitcher.

"I don't think so, Coach. It was a good pitch. That Ho just is a damn good hitter."

Hanson turned toward Roberto. "Okay, kid. I'm letting you run with this. But you let us know if you feel anything, okay?"

Annoyed, Roberto couldn't believe the fuss. He felt like saying, "Hey. I'm tossing a two-hit shutout, I've struck out fifteen batters, and this is what I get?" But instead he nodded his head. "Okay, Coach. Sure thing."

The next batter was Rudy Pagliano, the home-run leader of the league. Short, almost stocky, he didn't give Roberto the impression of being a powerful hitter. His first pitch, a fastball on the inside corner, made a believer of him.

Pagliano wheeled on the throw with a powerful shoulder turn. The compact swing made solid contact and sent a long, towering shot down the third-base line. It hooked foul and crashed into the light pole over four hundred feet from home.

"Wow! . . ." Roberto let out and wiped his forehead.

Lumpy ran out to the mound and scowled. "Do the words 'home-run champion' ring a bell with you, Ramirez? Keep it away from his sweet spot this time."

"I get the picture, man. I get the picture."

As Lumpy turned back to the plate, Roberto glanced over at the dugout. Pops was pacing.

Working from the stretch to keep Ho close at first, Roberto finessed two curve balls, one for a ball and one for a strike. The count was one and two. The curve balls did just the trick in upsetting Pagliano's timing. When Roberto returned to his fastball on the outside corner, it was an easy third strike.

Roberto punched the air with his fist.

"That's sixteen strikeouts for Ramirez tonight, tying the league record," the announcer blared.

The next batter took Roberto's first pitch and lofted a high fly ball toward third. Circling under it for what seemed an eternity, Vance Lee made the grab for the second out. There was only one more chance for Roberto to get the record.

"C'mon, Ramirez. You can do it!" the crowd screamed in encouragement.

The infielders surrounding Roberto chattered out their support as well.

"Fire it by him, Magic," Deek Slater yelled from second base.

"You can do it, man. Strike him out!"

Roberto quickly went to work. He blazed two of his best fastballs by the Padre hitter for two quick strikes. The crowd noise increased to a roar.

Pops Hanson moved to the top step of the dugout. Even he was caught up in the electricity of the moment.

Roberto went into the stretch. He paused and glanced over at first, then back to his catcher. He started his motion and to everyone's surprise . . . . spun and fired to first.

Danny Ho was caught flat-footed. The first baseman put an easy tag on him for the third out. The game ended 5–0 for the Dodgers, but the crowd stood in stunned silence. The whole team stood in stunned silence.

Roberto smacked his hand into his glove and jumped in the air. He started to trot toward the dugout. Finally his team came to life and rallied around him to congratulate him.

"Great game, Ramirez." "Fantastic pitching." "Wayda go, Ramirez. You're all right!"

When Pops Hanson reached him, he threw an arm around him and pulled him away from the crowd.

"Hey, Ramirez. Why'd you do that? You had the record in your hip pocket."

Roberto smiled. "Hey. That guy Ho got to me twice. I just wanted a little revenge. I knew I could catch him leaning over there. What can I say, Coach? It was the right play to make!"

"What about the record?"

"This was only my first game, Coach, remember?"

Hanson smiled. "You got that right, kid."

NINE

Glen Mitchell and David Green walked the three blocks from the ball park to Elmira's best burger establishment: Helvetia's. David had discovered it his second night in town and was now one of its most frequent customers. After his game-winning home run against Glen's White Sox, he was keeping his word and buying his friend a late-night snack.

The two former Rosemont Rocket stars slid into one of the booths by the front window. David waved to a couple of his teammates and winked when his favorite waitress spotted him.

"Diane, come on over," he said, waving at the cute, dark-haired waitress.

Glen flipped a sugar packet at him. "Hey, what's going on here? Who's that?"

"Hang on a minute. I'll introduce you. She's just a good friend . . . you know . . . like Lilian at Eat Burger back home."

Glen shook his head. "Yeah, right. This girl's dynamite looking . . . and about thirty years younger than Lilian."

"You'll never know, Mitchell."

The bright-eyed young waitress, in a white uniform with a red-and-blue-checked apron, suddenly appeared by their table. With a wide smile and perky voice, she said, "Hi, David. Good to see you!"

Glen leaned across the table and knuckle-punched David on the arm. "Eat here a lot, huh, David?"

"Every chance I get, guy." Turning back to Diane, David turned on his winning smile and irresistible charm. "Diane, I want you to meet my friend—"

"Scrapper? Right?" she said, finishing his sentence for him. "I've heard so much about you." She extended her hand in greeting. "I'm Diane Webster."

Glen stood up and smiled. "Hi. I hope some of the things you heard about me were good?"

Diane knew just how to play the two friends off of each other. "A few . . . but none from this guy," she said, nodding at David.

David grabbed for her arm but she side-stepped it easily.

Looking around for her boss, Diane moved closer and pulled out her order pad. "I'd better get back to work or I'll get in trouble. What can I get you hotshots?"

David ordered for both of them. "We want the Works, and a couple of shakes, one chocolate, one vanilla."

After Diane left, David turned back toward his friend. "Okay, Mitchell. Time to come clean."

"Me? What're you talking about?"

"That line drive I hit in the fifth. You should've gotten it."

Glen reached for a straw and spun the wrapper around with his fingers. "Hey, no big deal. I can't be perfect all the time. Even second-stringers like you get lucky."

David leaned across the table, his forearm raised. Glen met his forearm with his own in the Rosemont tradition.

"Got to agree with you this time. I've been lousy."

Glen turned serious. "I just think your stance got screwed up somewhere along the line. Ya know it's easy to fall into something and not even notice it."

"Yeah, well I fell into something, no question about it. I'm just glad *you* did. Damn, it felt good to get a hold of a pitch again."

"The important thing is to keep it going now."

The shakes came, and Diane winked at David as she put them on the table and left. David grabbed his shake and raised it in the air. "A toast," he exclaimed.

Glen met his glass with his.

"To a great season the rest of the way and a happy reunion back home in September . . . with Magic!"

"All right!"

With a great deal of difficulty, Glen slowly rolled open one eyelid as he tried to get his bearings. After a second of groggy uncertainty, he remembered he was on the bus. The familiar figure of Whiplash started to come into focus.

The long two-week road trip was finally coming to an end. Glen cleared his throat and hoarsely whispered out, "Where are we, Whiplash?"

Even after driving all night, Whiplash seemed alert and sharp. "Morning, Scrapper. You sleep well in these luxurious accomodations?"

"Oh, yeah," Mitchell said, stretching. "Just great."

"Well, you'll be happy to know that we's about half hour from home . . . or should I say Utica."

Shifting to an upright position, Glen tried to look out the bus window and get enough light to see his watch. Whiplash saw his struggle in the rearview window and flipped on the overhead aisle lights.

Glen saw that it was four-thirty in the morning. They'd left Watertown sometime the night before, Glen couldn't remember when, after a twilight doubleheader. They had to be home tonight in time for a game against Auburn.

"Say, Whiplash. Drive slow. I need about another eight hours' sleep."

"Sure thing. I'll take a detour and get you there in just enough time to suit up." Whiplash laughed.

Glen slid down in his seat and covered his head with his jacket.

When the bus pulled into the White Sox' parking lot the players slowly scrambled off and headed in various directions toward home. In eight hours they'd have to report back to the ball park for the next game.

Glen dragged himself up the flight of stairs to his small one-bedroom apartment. Fumbling with his keys, he barely got the door open, his bag flung on the ground and his head to the pillow before he fell asleep.

He had just settled into a sound slumber when the irritating ring of the doorbell woke him.

Glen grumbled and ignored it.

After the sixth ring, he cursed and stumbled to the door. Mad at the interruption, he yanked it open. "Dad! What . . ."

Joe Mitchell stood in the entryway, suitcase in hand. "Well? Can I come in or do I have to stand out here all day?"

Glen backed up and tried to shake the cobwebs from his head. "Sure . . . I mean, yeah, come on in. What are you doing here? I didn't know you were coming."

Joe looked around the room, nodding his head as if remembering something from long ago. "Boy, does this bring back memories. Probably a little nicer than my first place, but very similar."

The apartment was really just two rooms. A living room–kitchen-eating area, and a small bedroom with a tiny bath attached. The paint was peeling in a few places but basically it was clean and functional. Easily its best feature was the price.

Dropping his bag down on the end of the couch, Joe said, "It's pretty hard to get ahold of you when you're on the road. I had an opportunity to get away for a few days and wanted to come over here and see how you're doing."

Glen felt uncomfortable. "You didn't have to worry. I'm doing fine. We just got back from our road trip a couple of hours ago and I was getting some sleep."

"I understand. But you know your mom. She wanted some firsthand info. The kind she can't get from you over the phone."

Glen took a couple of steps toward the kitchen area. He shook his head again and squinted at the clock on the stove. "Can I get you anything, or—"

"Coffee, if you've got some."

Nodding his head, Glen reached up in the

cupboard. "Yeah. Believe it or not, I think there is some around here. Some of the players on the team drink it, and I don't know if they brought it over here or if it was left here. But I can make you a cup . . . it's instant."

"Fine."

After an uncomfortable silence while Glen fumbled around in the kitchen, he brought the coffee to his father and sat down. "So? What's your game plan? How long are you here in beautiful Utica?"

"I thought I'd stick around a couple of days . . ."

Glen rolled his eyes.

". . . take in a few of your games and see what's happening."

"Okay."

Joe easily detected the negative tone in his son's voice. "I won't cramp your style. I promise."

"Speaking of cramped, do you have a place to stay here or what?"

"I could manage on the couch here unless you've got an objection."

It was the last thing Glen wanted. "It won't be very comfortable, but if that's what you want—"

"Good. That's settled. Now, what time do you have to be at the ball park today?"

"Not till five. Our game's at seven-thirty."

"Then listen. If you need to get some sleep go back to bed. I'll do a little poking around town and sight-seeing stuff. You don't have to entertain me."

Stifling a yawn, Glen looked back toward his bedroom. "I think I'd better get a little more rest."

Joe grabbed his son's shoulder and shook it. "When you're on the road, sleeping in different beds all the time is tough enough to get used to. Forget about the bus."

Glen walked toward his bed. "I'll just leave the door unlocked so you can come and go as you please. Nothing to steal in here anyway."

"I'll catch you later, then," Joe Mitchell told his son.

As the front door closed, Glen dove into bed and closed his eyes. He tossed and turned for several minutes and found himself staring up the ceiling. "Shoot! I wonder what he's gonna pull while he's here? Why'd he have to show up now?"

He dozed off before he could answer his own question.

Pacing around his apartment, Glen checked out his watch one more time. "Ten to five. Where the heck is he?"

Glen had managed to sleep until two o'clock. Since then he'd straightened up his room and taken a load of clothes down to the laundromat. His father hadn't shown up yet.

"Well, damn! I can't wait any longer. I've got

to get to the ball park," he shouted as he picked up his carry bag and slammed the front door shut. "He's gonna have to make it there on his own."

As soon as Glen entered the noisy clubhouse, he figured out what was happening. "I should have known!" he groaned.

A group of players were clustered around Glen's dad. They hung on his every word while he told stories about the good old days. It was a scene that Glen had witnessed hundreds of times before.

The White Sox manager strolled over to Glen's locker. Ignoring his father, Scrapper was angrily pulling on his uniform while muttering under his breath.

"Your dad's quite a guy," Ted Holmes said. "He must have a million stories to tell."

"Make that two," Glen spat out.

Holmes knew immediately what the problem was. "Heard 'em all a few times, I take it."

"You could say that. He manages to always find a new group of listeners somehow. Even if he has to fly halfway across the country to do it."

"I'm sure he just came out to see you. He's just like any other proud father. You can't blame him for that."

"I guess." Glen concentrated on tying his cleats.

"Hey, why . . . how about introducing me?"

Glen stood up and pulled on his hat. "Don't

worry, Coach. He'll get around to it on his own." Then he took his glove and walked out to the field.

Utica battled the Erie Orioles for nine tough innings. The score seesawed back and forth until the White Sox put together a three-run rally in the ninth to pull out the victory. Glen's two-out, RBI single had kept the rally going and he scored the winning run.

As the team filed back into the clubhouse, raucously yelling and celebrating their win, they were met by Joe Mitchell. He had watched the game from behind the dugout, calling out advice and encouragement.

As they walked past him, he patted them and gave out high-fives. "Exciting game, guys. Good win! Wayda hang in there!"

Glen came in, scooted to the side of the clubhouse away from his father, and made his way to his own locker. After laughing and talking to the other players, Joe came and sat beside him.

"You looked pretty good out there, son," he said as he put an arm around Glen's shoulders.

Shrugging off his jersey top and his father's arm, Glen mumbled, "We won . . . that's the important thing."

"It's important to win, that's right. But don't forget that this is an individual fight for jobs, too. You've got to look good yourself."

"I'm doing all right."

Joe nodded. "Yeah. I'm sure you are. But you're still laying too far back in the batter's box. You didn't look aggressive up there."

Glen lost his cool. "I got two hits, three RBIs and scored twice. We won the game. And you still don't think I'm doing anything right?" He was yelling.

The clubhouse quieted for a minute as everybody looked over at the Mitchells.

In a soft voice Joe said, "Calm down. I didn't say that."

"That's what it sounded like to me!" Glen shouted.

The players turned away and went back to their own conversations.

Joe said, "Now listen. If you did what I told you, you would've driven that last ball down the line . . . coulda got extra bases probably. You'd pull the ball with more power."

"Well, I'm batting over three twenty-five my way."

"That doesn't mean there isn't a better way, does it?"

"It was good enough to help win the state championship, and I think it's gonna be good enough to help get me to the majors."

Joe Mitchell shook his head. "It's a simple change and won't disrupt your swing at all."

Glen jumped up and yelled through clenched teeth. "So what? I'm not interested in changing. The manager hasn't asked me to change. None of the other players have asked me to change. So why don't you just leave me alone?"

Joe stood staring into his son's fiery eyes. "Fine. I'm glad you got everything figured out. It was nice seeing you, too." He turned and walked out of the clubhouse.

Glen watched the retreat silently for a second, unsure of what to do. He crumpled up his jersey and threw it hard against the locker across from him. He sank back down on his bench, his head dropping down into his hands.

"Damn!" was all he could say.

of the other players have asked me to pitch in.

to write with someone. As the season was

TEN

"Another piece of pie, boys?" the waitress asked her two young customers.

"Naw . . . we'd better not. We've got a game in a few hours. Thanks, anyway."

Roberto Ramirez continued rifling through a copy of the *Sporting News*, anxiously looking for the minor-league stats section. Over the season, it had become his link back to his friends David and Glen. Besides an occasional phone call and a couple of postcards from strange little cities, this was the only way to tell how they were doing.

With only a few weeks left in the season, Roberto was getting anxious to return home. Luckily, his family called frequently to stay in touch, but it wasn't the same as seeing them. He also couldn't wait to compare notes with his high school buddies, DT and Scrapper.

Deek Slater faked a yawn and leaned back in his chair. "Okay, Ramirez. Let me have it. How great are they doing this week?"

Roberto knocked Deek's foot off the edge of the table and his leg crashed to the ground. "Better than you are, so zip it while I find 'em."

His finger ran up and down the page, looking for their names.

"There's Scrapper. . . . Geez, he's still batting—can you believe it—three twenty-five . . . That's phenomenal!"

Deek's ears pricked up. "Damn, he's good." A quick calculation of his own average made Salem's second baseman worry. "What parent team is he with again?"

"White Sox. You don't have to worry. He's even in a different league," Roberto laughed.

"Yeah, that's good. There's nobody in the National League system doing anything like that, is there?" Slater looked cross-eyed at his teammate.

Roberto ignored him. "Hey, that must be really something back in the New York–Penn League. Utica and Elmira are tied, only two games outta first behind Little Falls. Wouldn't it be great to be battling for a title right now?"

Deek smiled. "Instead of battling to stay outta the cellar, you mean?"

Roberto groaned. "Yeah, the clubhouse's like a graveyard lately. Everyone seems to just accept the losses."

"You're right. Nobody seems too upset about it. I guess the guys don't realize it makes it a lot harder to get noticed when you're on a loser. I just hope I'm not stuck down here again next year."

Nodding his head, Roberto shuddered at the thought. He'd had a great season by almost any measure. He was ten and three, with a 1.19 ERA. He was averaging an impressive 12.3 strikeouts for each nine innings worked. An average that was over three points higher than the greatest strikeout artist of all time, Nolan Ryan.

But, like Deek Slater mentioned, it was hard to get noticed on a losing team, and the Dodgers had certainly lost plenty. There were a mere 31 wins interspersed between their 64 losses.

"Hey, here's DT." Roberto called out as he pointed down at the page. "Wow. He's up to twenty-six home runs! That's leading the league!"

"Figures." Deek mumbled. "They grow 'em bigger, stronger, and faster in Rosemont . . . no doubt about it!"

Magic wacked the paper on his buddy's head. "C'mon. Let's get outta here. It must be time to get ready for the game."

Jumping up from his seat, Deek led the two of them out of the restaurant. "All right. Let's go make some statistics of our own. Whaddaya say?"

"Lead on, man. I'll follow."

The Salem Dodgers were at home for a game against the Everett Giants. Everett was in first place in the northern division of the league. Salem was in last place in the southern division.

Despite their disappointing win-loss record, Pops Hanson was happy with his team. He was used to measuring results in different ways than wins or losses. His job was to help teach and develop future major-league players. As he walked around the clubhouse before the game, he felt satisfied that he had done just that. Despite the losing record, Pops had kept everyone's energy level high and spirits strong.

"Okay, you guys. Listen up. You no doubt remember our last game against Everett up there, so I won't repeat any of the gory details. I just want you to go out there tonight and play your hardest and see if we can't get some revenge for that thumping we took."

A cheer went up in the locker room.

Pops smiled. "They're leading the league and this is our last chance against them this year. This is our play-off game so let's make the most of it."

Looking over at Roberto, he paused and then said, "Magic! Show no mercy tonight. Let's make this a game they'll never forget."

Throwing his fist in the air, Roberto yelled, "The Giants *must* die!"

The rest of the players screamed their agreement.

As he walked out to the mound to start the ball game, Roberto looked out at the time and temperature gauge across the street from the park. Standing on his tiptoes, he could just make out the flashing temperature: ninety-six degrees.

The Salem crowd seemed ready and eager for the heat and the game. Dressed in shorts, halter tops, and swimsuits, they cheered for the Dodgers, the home team. It was hat night and everyone in the stands was wearing the free Dodgers baseball cap they were given. It promised to be a special night.

Roberto carefully stepped over the white-chalked baseline. It was a superstition that he'd always respected. When he reached the mound he dug a toehold next to the rubber and then scraped a landing area for his front foot.

When the first Giant batter stepped into the box, Roberto peered in at Lumpy and winked.

"Let's do it," Lumpy yelled.

The infielders were fired up, too. With chants of support for Roberto and vicious insults for the batter, they seemed more motivated than ever before. Everything was in place for a good game.

Pops Hanson was impressed. He knew his

team was ready to play. "Okay, guys. Tonight's the night!"

Magic's first pitch was an effortless fastball that popped into Lumpy's glove for a strike. A curve ball and then the dreaded split-fingered fastball produced the first strikeout.

Whenever Roberto pitched, the fans along the first-base foul line hung little K's over the fence to signify each strikeout. The first white cardboard square with its black K was now hanging.

At the end of the first inning there were three.

Salem's problems all season long were centered around their hitting. Even in the games that Magic had lost, he'd pitched well enough, but gotten no support. Pops Hanson knew tonight was going to be different.

The first Dodger batter singled. The second batter, Deek Slater, doubled off the left-field wall. A walk, another single, and a home run produced an immediate 5–0 lead. With Roberto on the mound, Salem's manager sat back and smiled. He'd already gotten all the runs he would need.

As the game moved on, the only drama unfolding was the lengthening string of K's hung over the fence. After six innings they totaled thirteen. With the score now 11–0, the crowd focused on the excitement on the mound.

Roberto sat next to Pops on the bench. "Well, Coach, looks like your pep talk worked. This is the best we've played since I've been here."

"Maybe I should have gotten on you guys earlier. What do ya think?"

Roberto shrugged. "I think you've been great all year. A few hits in the right places and our record would be a lot different."

"Right. But there's one thing I'd like to see come outta this season." Pops's eyes honed in on Roberto's.

"Yeah? What?"

"Well . . . I'd kinda like to see you get that record tonight, Magic. It's a great night to do it: the weather, the crowd, playing against the league champs, the whole bit. It would top off the season—for you and the team."

Roberto blushed. "Thanks, Coach. I'll try my best."

Hanson broke into a chuckle. "At least throw to that seventeenth batter if you get a chance. Don't go picking somebody off base again. Okay?"

"You got it, Coach!"

In the seventh inning, Roberto fanned the first batter, but the next two managed to fly out. In the eighth, he got two more K's, so the string reached sixteen.

As he took the mound for the ninth inning, Roberto received a standing ovation. Goose bumps ran down his spine. All of the infielders came in to the mound and patted him on the back and gave him words of encouragement. The stage was set for his run at the record.

Lumpy flashed him a sign for a fastball, and Roberto responded with the first strike. A beautiful curve ball moved the count to oh and two.

Trying to make a perfect pitch, Magic missed the outside corner of the plate with a fastball. He flipped his glove against his leg and kicked at the ground.

He threw a curve that bounced into the dirt for ball two. When the batter let his split-fingered fastball break down low for ball three, Roberto was obviously rattled.

Calling time, Lumpy ran out to the mound.

"Hey, Magic, look over behind the third-base dugout."

Confused, Roberto turned and quickly surveyed the area. "So? . . . I don't get it," he answered impatiently.

Lumpy punched him in the chest with his oversized glove. "Hey . . . c'mon, man. You're not dead yet, are you? Check out the blonde with the blue leotard on. Tell me she isn't dynamite!"

Roberto glanced over one more time and smiled. He nodded his head and pushed his catcher back toward home. "Get outta here, Lumpy. She's out of your league!"

Halfway back to the plate, the catcher whisked around and yelled, "Let's get outta here and we'll just see."

"In your dreams, pal."

Lumpy returned to his position behind the plate. His job was done. The tension in Roberto's pitching motion vanished as quickly as it had appeared. The third strike went by the batter before he decided to swing.

"Ladies and gentlemen, Roberto Ramirez has just broken the Northwest League record for strikeouts in a game with seventeen. Let's all give him a big hand!" the public-address announcer said.

His teammates came in from every position and off the bench to congratulate him out on the mound. Roberto tipped his hat to the crowd and then waited for the commotion to settle down. To top things off, he struck out the last two batters, finishing with nineteen and a three-hit shutout.

After the reporters finally left the locker room, Pops Hanson stopped by. "Nice work, kid. I'm proud of you."

"Thanks, Coach. It was your inspiration that did it."

Hanson laughed and waved him away. "Don't spread it too deep, Magic. I forgot my shovel. See you tomorrow."

"Night, Coach."

Deek Slater was the last to get to him. As the two of them walked out of the clubhouse into the warm night air, the second baseman said,

"Well, Magic, remember our conversation before the game?"

"Yeah . . . I guess so. Why?"

Deek slapped him on the back. "You sure as hell did something about getting noticed now, didn't you?"

Magic looked up and saw the bright array of stars in the sky. All he did was smile.

ELEVEN

David Green rounded third and headed for home in his now-famous home-run trot. The Elmira crowd cheered wildly as he hit the plate and tipped his hat toward the stands. David's round-tripper gave the home team Red Sox a come-from-behind 4–3 win over the St. Catherines Blue Jays.

Even more important, the win gave Elmira a share of first place in the league. Tied with Oneonta's Yankees, both teams were one game up on Glen's Utica White Sox. The race was going to come down to the last game.

David's slow start at the plate had given way to a fantastic flurry. During the last two months of the season, he'd smashed a league-leading twenty-six home runs. With only two games left, the Sox were closing in on a pennant.

"Wayda go, Green," Frank Brogan yelled as he entered the dugout. "Whata shot!"

David slapped high-fives with him. "Thanks, Brogie. We're still in it, two games to go!"

"It's been awhile since Elmira's been involved in a pennant race. I'll tell ya that."

"And I've gotta thank you for helping me out. If you wouldn't have taught me how to lay off the scroogie, I'd still be the laughingstock of this league."

"Just doin' my job, kid."

As the two of them walked from the dugout toward the clubhouse, other teammates slapped hands and congratulated him. When he reached his cubicle in the locker room, he sat down to relax but was surprised by a familiar voice.

"DT Green." Jeff Fox punched him on shoulder. "Wayda go out there!"

"What're you doing in here, boss? Who let you outta the front office?" David was surprised to see the owner's son.

"Hey, I had to come down and see you . . . and to let you know. . . ." His voice rose as he motioned the other players to gather around David's locker.

Elmira's center fielder looked suspicious. "Hey, what's going on here?"

Jeff pretended to be serious . . . but failed. "The official scorekeeper-statistician—record-book keeper—water cooler monitor—in other words, me—has determined that the Elmira Red Sox have a new all-time, single-season, home-run champion!"

The clubhouse broke into loud cheering.

Jeff held up his hands for quiet. "I have to admit, there are a few seasons where the records aren't exactly clear, but I'm reasonably sure, from everything I can dig up, that twenty-seven dingers represents a milestone in Elmira's long history. Congratulations, DT. You've been an inspiration to the whole team!"

Johnny Sullivan approached David's locker while the team roared its approval. He held up one hand and the room immediately became quiet.

"First, I want to add my congratulations to Jeff's; for Green and the rest of you guys. This year has been one of the most exciting I can remember." Sullivan looked around, smiling. "But, we've got some work ahead."

"Yeah, Coach, two more games to win!" Dick Storey, the right fielder shouted.

"Right!" Sullivan shouted back. "Then what!"

"The pennant!" the whole team yelled.

"That's right. The first for Elmira, and you guys are gonna win it!"

The clubhouse exploded in cheers.

The St. Catherines Blue Jays were a strong team that had run into a slump. But each player was still striving for that stellar performance that would help catapult him higher in the minor-league system.

St. Catherines jumped out to a quick 3–0 lead against the Red Sox in the finale. It was a bunch of grim-faced players who stumbled into the dugout after that first inning.

"C'mon guys, fire up out there!" Coach Sullivan yelled. "Don't tell me you're ready to roll over and play dead?"

"No way, Coach!" DT hollered back. "We'll get 'em, don't worry."

But the Elmira coach had plenty of reason to worry. The Blue Jays' starting pitcher was a crafty left-hander with a blistering fastball. After five innings, the Sox hadn't managed a single hit.

Frank Brogan walked up and down the dugout between innings, reminding his players to relax up at the plate. He explained how the tension was killing them and making the Jays' pitcher even more effective.

"You guys have to slow everything down when you go up there," he lectured. "Take a deep breath . . . make slow, easy practice swings. You're trying too hard and your timing's shot. Slow it down."

The players numbly nodded their heads. But they continued to parade to the plate and become easy outs. Going to the bottom of the eighth, Elmira saw their dream fading away, still behind 3–0.

Brogie and Coach Sullivan looked at the

batting order for the eighth and knew this was their last chance. After the pitcher hit, the top of the order was coming up. Sullivan nodded his head and said, "It's now or never, Brogie."

"Keep your fingers crossed."

Elmira's first batter worked hard, fouling off several pitches before managing a walk. He was only their third base runner.

When the next batter, Jerry Sanders, hit a routine ground ball down toward third, Sullivan and Brogan groaned. But the Jays' player scooped up the ball and fired it over the second baseman's head into right field for an error, and suddenly the Sox had runners on second and third. The whole dugout came alive, cheering and screaming for a rally.

"Let's go, Sox! Let's go!" "Big inning!" "One time . . . one time!"

St. Catherines's pitcher, Felix Dejoux, answered the call. With three pitches, he struck out the next batter. A painful groan emerged from the Sox dugout.

When the next batter hit a high chopper back to the mound, everyone thought it was curtains for the Sox. Dejoux waited for the high bouncer to come down, gloved it, and checked the runner on third to make sure he wasn't going. By the time he turned and fired to first, Mark Brown had beaten it out for a base hit.

David clapped his hands and hollered encouragement to his teammates. He moved down the length of the dugout, slapping hands and pumping everyone up. He grabbed his bat and navy blue batting helmet and moved into the on-deck circle.

"Let's go, Sox! Keep it going, Chaney!" he yelled.

St. Catherines's manager jumped out of the dugout and ran to the mound. After a brief conference with his pitcher and catcher, he decided to leave him in.

His confidence in Dejoux was justified. Bearing down hard, the Jays' hurler fired two fastballs and a wicked curve by Lonzell Chaney to get the second strikeout of the inning.

The Elmira fans let down for a moment until they saw it was David Green walking to the plate. A loud wave of clapping and cheering built to a fever pitch as their home-run champion approached the batter's box.

"Now batting for the Sox . . . David Green!" The P.A. announced.

Everyone was on their feet, screaming.

Sullivan and Brogie moved to the top step of the dugout. They looked at each other for a fleeting second. They could feel the electricity in the air. They knew everything was in place for a storybook finish. They hoped.

When St. Catherines's manager saw that it was DT moving into the batter's box, he called his catcher over to the dugout. After a quick talk, the catcher came back and went out to the mound.

David dug in at the plate and waited.

When the Jays' catcher took his position, David took a couple of practice swings and set himself for the pitch. But when the pitcher went into his stretch, the catcher bounced up and took a step away from the plate. The pitcher threw to him way outside.

David stood in stunned silence, staring at the catcher.

The crowd went delirious, screaming and yelling like a lynch mob.

"They're gonna walk him with the bases loaded and give us a token run. Damn!" Brogie said, slamming his hat down to the ground.

Sullivan shook his head. "Smart play on ol' Bill Morelli's part. . . . I've gotta hand it to 'im! But I ain't falling for it!" Sullivan jumped up and ran toward the home-plate umpire. "Hey ump, time out here. Time out!"

The coach stood at the plate facing David but was yelling straight at the St. Catherines dugout. "You lousy, no-good cowards! Let's play ball here! What is this bull? You've got your best pitcher up there. Let's see what he's got!" He was trying to goad them into action.

The umpire stepped in front of the enraged manager. "That's enough, Johnny. Get back in the dugout!"

"Not until I get them to play ball here. What's this crap walking a man with the bases loaded?"

"Perfectly legal, Sullivan. You know that. Now, get outta here. Play ball," the ump yelled.

Sullivan turned back toward his dugout. The

crowd started booing loudly again, and the Sox'
manager pumped his arms up and down encour-
aging the mayhem. Soon, the Blue Jays' dugout
was getting pelted with debris.

Popcorn boxes, peanut bags, paper cups, and
ice cream sticks were getting hurled onto the
playing field in protest. When the catcher took
his position outside the plate again, the booing
was so loud David couldn't hear himself think.

After the second intentional ball, the umpire
called time. The field had become so covered
with garbage that play had to be suspended to
clean it up. He went over to the press box and
spoke to Jeff Fox.

Jeff got on the P.A. system and told the crowd
that the game might be forfeited if they didn't
stop their outrageous display. His announce-
ment was met by the loudest booing of the day.

Finally, St. Catherines's manager went out to
the plate to talk to his catcher. "Set up normally
and just make sure that your target is well
outside. The crowd will think we've given in and
quiet down. Okay?"

The catcher agreed on the plan, and the game
was resumed. The crowd cheered wildly when
they saw the St. Catherines catcher in a normal
position behind the plate.

Sullivan turned to Brogie. "They're not fool-
ing me for a second. I bet this pitch bounces up
to the plate."

Brogie was watching his star hitter standing
out in the box. Seemingly oblivious to the

commotion around him, David's eyes seemed to be boring in on the pitcher. Brogie saw the stare and said to the manager, "For that pitcher's sake, it'd better!"

Dejoux had gone into his stretch and fired his third pitch.

Almost a foot off the outside corner of the plate, the pitch was a waist-high fastball that would move the count to 3–0. But the throw looked good enough to David.

Stepping into the pitch and reaching his thirty-six–ounce bat out across the plate, David unleashed a ferocious cut. The fat part of the bat met the fastball squarely, and the ball shot off from the flame-tempered ash and tore through the sky like a missile.

The Elmira fans had seen a lot of impressive home runs by their young star. But he'd saved his best for last. Mesmerized, the crowd stood silently watching as the ball started to disappear even before they knew what had happened.

When the cheer finally broke out, the Sox faithful started jumping up and down and hugging each other. The entire Elmira bench rose up in one huge charge toward their hero.

As he circled the bases, David kept his eye on the flight of the ball, watching it disappear over a building across the street from the left-field wall. A million thoughts flooded through his mind as he tipped his cap toward the crowd.

Elmira's pennant chances now rested with a

4–3 lead that had to be protected in the top of the ninth. The Red Sox hurler, Francisco Javier, quickly took out the first two batters. But, pumped up by the crowd's cheers, he overthrew his next four pitches and walked a man. With two down, top of the ninth, a runner on first, and a chance at the pennant, the Elmira crowd was on its feet again.

David watched his pitcher struggle with two more balls. He knew he'd have to come in with a sweet pitch pretty soon to end the string of non-strikes. On the next pitch, that's what happened.

St. Catherines's batter saw the fastball coming right down the middle of the plate and got excited. He swung and smashed a towering high fly ball toward straightaway center field.

David picked up the flight of the ball and started racing backward toward the fence. When his feet hit the warning track, he knew the ball was going to be a foot or two over the fence.

Planting himself for a desperation leap, Green watched for the ball's descent. Then he soared up into the air, his glove stabbing at the ball just as it was about to disappear over the fence. David speared the ball, made the catch, crashed into the wall, but held on for the final out.

David jumped up to his feet and held the ball high for everyone to see. The fans went delirious. Arms raised in victory, he ran in to join the wild celebration.

TWELVE

Glen Mitchell checked his airplane ticket again and then stuffed it into his bag. Glancing around his tiny apartment, he made sure that he had everything. When he pulled the door closed he locked it and then put the key back in through the mail slot. He wasn't going to need this place again.

Racing to the ball park, Scrapper was on a tight schedule. It was the final game of the season for the Utica White Sox. The game was scheduled for five o'clock. His plane was scheduled for eight-thirty.

A win would put them in a three-way tie for first with Oneonta and Elmira. Because of the head-to-head records of those three teams, Oneonta would win the title. It Utica lost, Elmira

123

and Oneonta would tie for first, with Elmira winning the title because of tie breakers.

The bad news is we're out of it, Glen thought as he raced across the parking lot toward the clubhouse. *I guess a tie for first sounds better than nothing, even though we won't win the title. Of course, if we lost . . .* He knew his friend David's team would win the pennant.

Utica got involved in a typical White Sox game . . . a low-scoring, defensive struggle. With little power on their team, the Sox were used to scratching and clawing for every run they got. It was a style that seemed to fit the player who had become their leader . . . Glen Mitchell.

Battling the Hamilton Cardinals tooth and nail throughout the game, Utica came up in the tenth with the score tied 1–1. Glen looked at the clock on the center-field scoreboard and saw it was seven-twenty.

"I'm gonna get all screwed up here with plane connections if we don't end this pretty soon." He paced up and down the dugout and tried to pump up his teammates. "C'mon, guys. Let's do it now! One run . . . all we need is one run."

The first batter in the bottom of the tenth struck out meekly and Glen rolled his eyes. As he walked to the plate he thought about trying to end it with one big hit.

Power wasn't the name of Scrapper's game, but he got a pitch he liked and gave it a rip. He connected just right and the ball soared out toward left field. The left fielder drifted back until he found himself up against the wall. Leaping high, he just missed as the ball bounced off the wall just beyond his reach.

With the ball bounding back toward the infield, Scrapper raced around first and headed for second. By the time the center fielder, backing up the play, reached the ball, Glen put his head down and headed for third.

The ball and Glen reached the base at the same split second, but the tag came down just after his fingers tickled the bag.

"Safe!" hollered the umpire.

The crowd roared its approval.

Glen danced around the bag nervously as the next batter dug in at the plate. When Hamilton's pitcher fired a strike by Lou Cabratza, Scrapper impatiently slammed his foot to the ground.

"Hey, Red," Mitchell said, calling the third-base coach over. "I'm going home on the next pitch! Signal Lou to lay down a bunt."

"You're crazy," Red replied.

"Come on, Red. This pitcher's too slow on the uptake. It'll work."

Red looked at the pitcher, then nodded and flashed the series of signs, and Lou stepped back into the box. The pitcher started his windup and Scrapper broke for the plate.

Startled, the Cards' pitcher changed his intended pitch from a curve ball to a fastball, trying to beat Glen's dash toward the plate. Lou squared around and made contact but the bunt bounced back directly to the pitcher.

"Damn!" Glen muttered as he tore toward home. "This is gonna be close!"

Diving headfirst, Scrapper slid under the tag into a cloud of dust. The umpire flashed his call and yelled out, "Safe!"

It had worked—a perfectly executed squeeze play.

The Utica team jumped up and down with excitement. The win gave them a share of first place for the season. They wouldn't be able to claim the pennant, but it felt great to know they were tied for first.

Ted Holmes worked his way through the crowd and found his second baseman. "Nice work, Mitchell. Even if you didn't clear it first."

"Thanks, Coach," Glen said as he walked toward the clubhouse.

"I know you've got a plane to catch, so just let me say, best of luck next year . . . wherever you wind up."

Glen shook hands with his manager and then hugged him. "Thanks again—for everything!" Waving to the rest of the guys, he ran for the locker room.

Robert Ramirez sat in the living room laughing and talking with his parents. He'd arrived home from Salem after a fabulously successful season. Unable to get away to see any of their son's games, the Ramirez family eagerly listened to every detail as he recalled his year with the Dodgers.

"So what's the most important thing you learned this summer, Robbie?" his mother asked him.

"Besides how to avoid going to the laundromat as much as possible, you mean?" he joked.

"Yes. Now be serious."

"I think the work I did on the slider is really going to help me. There are lots of fastball hitters and, from what I've heard, they're better and better as you move up the system. So you've got to have some pitches to fool 'em and keep 'em off balance."

Rosa Ramirez nodded. "You've always had a good curve ball, son. Wasn't it good enough?"

"Oh, yeah. That's no problem. Coach Hanson said my curve ball was really good. It's just that each additional pitch you've got in your bag makes it that much tougher for the hitter to be guessing on you up at the plate. Some of these hitters are so good that if they know what you're gonna throw, they can really tee off on it."

Carlos Ramirez listened intently. He'd waited the whole time for some mention of Roberto's plans for the future.

"Roberto?"

"Yeah, Dad?"

"What about school this fall? Does the team still intend to pay your way through college?"

Roberto sunk down in his seat. "I forgot to find out about that."

Angry, Carlos stood and walked toward his den. "Maybe I'd better get out that copy of the contract and look into that."

"Wait, Dad. Listen. The club is supposed to call me in the next few days and discuss what I should be doing in the off season to get ready for next year. They do that after they decide where everyone should be assigned. I can ask them then. It shouldn't be more than a week or so."

"And where do you stand?" Carlos asked his son.

"Whaddaya mean, Dad?"

"Do you still intend to go to school?"

Caught up in the excitement of playing ball, Roberto hadn't thought about college at all. He stretched the truth when he said, "Sure. I've been looking forward to it."

Carlos sat back down and relaxed. "Good. Baseball isn't forever, you know. You should remember that and use this opportunity as a means to an end. You shouldn't give up your lifelong dreams for it. The world will always need good doctors. I'm not so sure the same can be said about ballplayers."

Roberto meekly nodded. "Right, Dad."

Rosa interrupted the exchange between father and son. "Robbie . . . now tell me again. You said you set a new league record for strikeouts in a game?"

Turning animatedly toward his mother, Roberto smiled broadly. "Yeah, Mom. I struck out nineteen in my last game. It was terrific. I wish you could have been there. In the last inning of . . ."

Carlos watched his son carefully. He could see where the fire and determination in his son's life was now directed.

Tony La Russo looked up from the pile of papers on his desk. It was the first day back in school for teachers at Rosemont High and he had a million things to do to get ready for the start of school. As he grumbled about the mess in his office, he was surprised to hear three familiar voices approaching from the hallway.

"Whaddaya bet, he's not even in his office," Glen Mitchell said to his two friends.

David Green laughed. "Yeah. He's probably in the gym devising some new form of torture for his PE classes."

Roberto Ramirez disagreed. "Naw. He's so dedicated that I'm sure he's been here since seven-thirty this morning organizing his office for the year. Everything will be in its place and he'll be there preparing lessons for the whole year."

Recognizing the source of the voices, La Russo stood up and went to the door to greet his former stars. When their eyes met, a feeling of love and respect radiated out. "Well, look what the wind blew in." They shook hands all around. "I was wondering if you guys would ever show your faces around here again . . . now that you're big stars."

"Hey, you'll never get rid of us, Coach," DT corrected him.

"We knew you couldn't get along without us," said Scrapper.

"And I don't even want to try. So how you guys doing? How'd the season go for you?"

The boys filled him in on every detail of their successful minor-league season. In each boy's case, they managed to find an example of how La Russo's teachings and wisdom had helped them in a crucial situation. The Rockets' coach sat back in his chair beaming.

"Aw, you guys are all right, ya know that? I knew you'd have a good year." La Russo chuckled and said, "You've been coached too darn well, that's it!"

"He hasn't lost any of his humility, has he, guys?" Roberto asked.

La Russo stood and led the boys out of the office. They walked out on to their old practice field at Rosemont as they continued to talk.

"So what's the plan for next year?" their former manager asked.

A collective sigh went up. "That's what we don't know yet," said David. "We expect the word any day now. We're all kinda on pins and needles waiting to hear."

"Any guesses?"

Glen shook his head. "Naw. We just all hope that it's not A ball again. The money isn't very good and—"

La Russo cut him off. "Whoa now . . . the money isn't any good? What happened to those big signing bonuses you guys got? Don't tell me you haven't got any money?"

David punched La Russo. "C'mon, Coach. You know better than that. We're talking about the travel money for food and stuff. I've eaten so many Big Macs that I think I'm growing curly red hair and a big red nose."

Roberto chimed in, "Yeah. The traveling and the food aren't much fun, Coach. Most of the cities with A teams are pretty small. I think we'd all like to keep moving upward rather than spend another year at that level."

"For sure," said Glen. "My dad never did spend any time in Triple A. I suppose that's too much to hope for in this day and age. A straight shot to the majors would be nice, though."

"Dream on," laughed David. "You'd just better hope there's Double A in your future . . . and not a waiver notice!"

Glen's back went up. "Hey, I batted over three twenty-five and had fourteen game-winning hits. What're you talkin' 'bout waivers?"

David stood to his full six-foot-five-inch height and peered down at Glen. "Twenty-eight home runs, eighty-three RBIs, *fifteen* game-winning hits! Take that!"

"Okay, okay. That's enough," laughed Roberto. "You guys were both lucky you didn't have to face any good pitchers . . . like me!"

La Russo turned and walked back toward the school building. "It's getting too deep for me, guys. But why don't you come back tomorrow morning? School doesn't start for another couple of days and I'm having an informal game with some of the guys who'll be on this year's team. It might be fun to have you *stars* here."

"Sounds great," they echoed, and off they ran.

The next morning, Coach La Russo stood at home plate hitting fungos to his Rocket infielders. He heard screaming and yelling and stopped to watch three boys come running onto the field. Each clutched a yellow piece of paper in their hands.

David, Glen, and Roberto all reached La Russo at the same time. They all tried to talk at once. The gibberish that followed was inaudible.

"Hey, slow down. What the heck's going on here," he said.

The former Rosemont heroes looked at each other and saw they were all clutching the same type of yellow form. Glen figured it out first. "Assignments came today from the parent club, Coach. It looks like everyone's gotten sent out at the same time."

Roberto nodded breathlessly.

David gulped out, "You got it!"

They looked at each other for a silent second and then simultaneously said, "Well?"

"I'll go first," Glen said. He held up his telegram and read, "Report for spring training with the parent club . . . in Florida . . . February Second!"

Roberto and David jumped straight up in the air.

"Same here!" screamed Roberto.

"Me, too," said David.

Coach La Russo rubbed their heads and slapped them on the back. "Wayda go, guys. That's terrific!"

"We're going to the bigs!" yelled Glen.

"I'll be pitching to major-league batters," said Roberto.

"A shot at the big time . . . fantastic," hollered David.

La Russo hid his smile by clearing his throat. "Okay, you hotshots," he said, lifting the bat to his shoulder. "We got a game starting here. You guys ready or what?"

"You know it, Coach!" the three rookies shouted together and headed for their old high school ball field.

Follow our hotshot ROOKIES as they shatter team records on their way to the majors in:

ROOKIES #3: SPRING TRAINING